By Jack Farris

Novels

Ramey

A Man To Ride With

Me and Gallagher

The Abiding Gospel of Claude Dee Moran Junior

Drama

Into Thy Narrow Bed

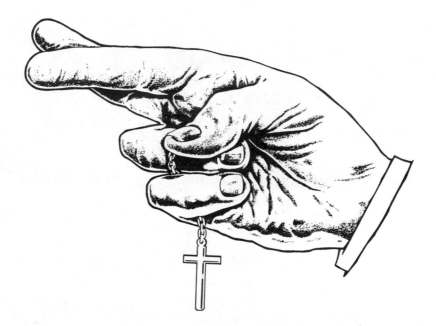

A NOVEL BY JACK FARRIS

The Abiding Gospel of Claude Dee Moran, Jr.

St. Luke's Press
1987

LIBRARY OF CONGRESS
CATALOGING-IN-PUBLICATION DATA
Farris, Jack, 1921-
    The Abiding Gospel of Claude Dee Moran, Jr.

I. Title.
PS3556.A776 5A63 1987 813'.54 86-297 03
ISBN 0-018 518-52-0

Jacket design by Larry Pardue

For information address: St. Luke's Press, Suite 401,
    Mid-Memphis Tower, 1407 Union, Memphis, TN 38104

For Linton and Jan, with love

PART ONE

THE REVIVALIST

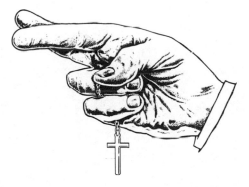

King Solomon loved many strange women.

1 Kings XI,1

Life is the art of drawing sufficient conclusions from insufficient premises.

Samuel Butler

True, I ain't been saved by a regular preacher, but I sure as hell been born again.

Claude Dee Moran Junior

Chapter One

Name's Claude Dee Moran Junior. Served time up at
Pordell prison, four years, seven months, and some odd
days. Charged with second degree murder, which I done.
Shot dead my best friend Larry Lee Ludlow. Come home
from squirrel hunting caught him messing around with
my Ada, fucking my never loving wife in my own bed on
my green percale sheets. Run to the backporch for my
shotgun, Larry Lee stayed to put on his britches. His last
mortal mistake. Cut him down with a single blast, a
spooked rabbit running a jagged lope down the wagon
lane into a sweet sunset. Seen his body jerk once and fall
face down in the dust.

Like the gospel says, to dust ye shall return.

Come home from Pordell on a hot Sunday afternoon in June. Rode the bus to Highsville and walked her in from there, six miles from nowhere to nowhere with nothing but the clothes on my back and one lonesome sawbuck in my pocket.

Could a told you, found Ada gone, leaving nothing but a twenty acre hardtack farm streaked with gulley washes, yard peckerdeep in buckleweed, and a dominicker hen ruffling in the dirt under the front steps. Wondering same as me I reckon what the hell she was doing there.

Didn't surprise me none, Ada being gone. She was always a far roamer with a slant look and a reckless ass. Hair the color of sunlit marigolds, eyes brown as honeycomb in the hive. Had the heart of a whore but I loved her dear. Times she loved me back.

Went around to the backyard, found more devastation. A sagging fence with rotted posts running half the length of what used to be the garden, separating nothing from nothing, a live hornets' nest hanging in a blackjack sprout by the wellporch, a hunkered down bluetick hound with a gimpy hind leg and a tucked in tail, slinking off towards the sumac behind the barn lot.

Grabbed a clod of dirt and chunked the hound, then sit down on the back steps and done some pretty serious thinking.

First thought, Claude Dee, you ain't nothing but a poor misbegotten sonofabitch without the chance of a snowball in hell.

Next thought, shit, boy, try to pull yourself together, whining is for women and old folks, ain't nobody going to pick you up but your ownself.

Sit a good little while watching the sun slide slow across the sky towards Butternut mountain, hazy blue in the distance, thought, boy, that sun and them mountains don't give a good rat's ass about your problems or nobody else's. That give me the nerve to go on in.

Inside the house nothing but empty closets, a stripped bed, a coffee pot on the stove with live moss growing inside. Half the windows busted out, a clogged commode, dried rat turds on the kitchen table, a calendar on the wall with a sweet picture of Jesus carrying in his arms a wounded lamb.

Be it never so humble.

Went down to the creek behind the willow grove, took myself a hobo bath, set out for town. Walked the fields off the main road, come in at the railroad siding below the cotton gin, took a left turn at Newberry's blacksmith shop.

Seen old man Newberry under the leanto nailing a shoe on the hind leg of a brindle mule. Married Princey Belle Barnes when he was seventy-two, her not yet twenty. She borned him or somebody a son, which he named Big Boy. Hammered in the last nail, sit the hoof down easy, then seen me walking along the road. Thinks, damned if that ain't old Claude Dee Moran Junior, back from the pea farm. Come a step forward, hand over his eyes, waved me a halfway hello.

I kept on a walking, head down, counting the bitterweed dividing the wheel ruts. Not yet ready to renew my acquaintance with a broke dick old man, stone deaf in one ear and hard a hearing in the other.

Turned the corner, three houses on down come to that privet hedge I trimmed many a time when just a kid of a boy.

There she sit on the front porch, seemed like same as I left her four years, seven months, and some odd days ago. A weazily little woman, prune-faced and pucker-mouthed, rocking slow, eyes closed, a sweetgum snuffstick hanging out the side of her mouth.

My Aunt Heather, as sweet a sight as ever I seen.

I come walking up she opened her eyes, leaned a little forward squinting against the dying sunlight, said, "Claude Dee Moran Junior?"

I said, "Yes, mam, Aunt Heather, it's me."

She said, "Let you out did they?"

I said, "Yes, mam, done my time like a man, come home to make something of myself."

She said, "Nothing to make from. You was always worthless as tits on a boar hog."

I said, "No, mam, I ain't the same as I was when they took me off to the pen. I done a lot of thinking while I was locked up. Took to reading the bible, done some pretty serious praying. Even took a course in the all time greatest books ever wrote. You ain't looking at the same Claude Dee Junior you took in and raised from a boy."

"And lived many a time to regret," she said. Leaned back, closed her eyes, went on rocking. After a little, said, "Sit."

So I sit. The sun was going down, streaking the yard with purple shadows, a little breeze stirring. I closed my eyes and let my mind run free and it was like I hadn't never been away. Like I hadn't never met and married Ada and busted my ass working three jobs at once to pay off that chinkapin farm or caught Ada fondly fucking Larry Lee and shot dead my best friend, or sit up there at Pordell marking off days on the wall and yearning for just one breath of free air.

It was like I was back a boy again, just me and Aunt Heather, sitting on the porch late of an afternoon shelling peas, with dusk coming down easy and the locusts singing sweet in the mulberry tree.

"I reckon you're hungry," Aunt Heather said.

I said I reckoned I was, hadn't eat nothing since noon the day before, nothing then but a moon pie and a RC cola.

She made a mournful sound, said, "Merciful Redeemer, another mouth to feed." Hoisted herself out of the chair, talking to herself said, "God's mean to old folks."

Going in that house near about brought tears to my eyes. Things I'd put myself to sleep thinking about up at Pordell many a night, I ain't ashamed to say. The clock on the wall with Jesus Saves wrote across the face. The bowl of wax pears I give Aunt Heather on her sixty-first birthday. Picture of Uncle Edgar dressed in his army uniform on a table in the corner. Give his life for his country in a truck wreck somewheres in France during the war. A two-timing sonofabitch, born with a hard on, but love's a jigsaw puzzle. Aunt Heather never stopped pining for him, remembering him better than he was.

She heated up some poke salad, fried a mess of salt pork, cooked a skillet of crackling bread, said for me to give the blessing.

I said, "Thank you, Lord, for chastising me for what I done. Also for this bountiful feast. As you can plainly see, ain't nobody cooks like my Aunt Heather."

Aunt Heather said pshaw and sit down. Sit a little watching me eat, said, "You give any thought to how you aim to make a living?"

I said, "Yes, mam, give it quite a lot of thought. Got it narrowed down to raising chickens or revival preaching."

Thought she couldn't a heard right, said, "Revival preaching!"

I said, "Yes, mam, been called to it. Heard the wind and the Lord wasn't in it. Heard the earthquake and the Lord wasn't in that. Heard the fire and the Lord wasn't in that either. Then heard the still, small voice. Book of Kings, chapter ten."

She said, "Claude Dee Junior, you done addled your brain reading so much. You can't preach, lessen you're ordained."

I said, "Yes, mam, I thought about that. And the way I figure it is, you dress like a preacher, walk like a preacher, talk like a preacher, ain't nobody going to ask are you a preacher."

She shook her head, said, "Lordamercy, boy, you ain't even been saved."

I said, "Same as. Two of them guards up at Pordell took a disliking to my face, damn near beat all the meanness out of me. It's true I ain't been saved by a regular preacher but I sure as hell been born again."

She give that a little thought, said, "The Lord works in mysterious ways."

We done the dishes and she got to talking about my daddy and mama and how I come to be left in her care, a mere five year old waif.

And how that was was, my daddy got decapitated by a snapped winchline and two weeks later my mama run off with Muley Duggan. A one-eyed hog farmer twenty years older than her, who left behind a fuckedout tubercular wife and eight ratty-assed kids. All about the same age, Aunt Heather said. Said mama brought me to her door on a cold December morning, said mama said, "Sister, I ain't got nobody else to turn to, you'll have to take the boy to raise. He ain't Claude Dee's son and he ain't Muley's son, but there ain't no bad blood in him, you got my word on that."

Aunt Heather said she never seen mama again and never heard nothing from her but only just once. Wrote a letter about a year later, said she'd left Muley and was working as a hostess in the Texas Hotel in Miami.

Aunt Heather didn't say no more about that and neither did I. Having a mama turned to whoring ain't something you care to dwell on.

All the time Aunt Heather was talking I was trying to think how to say what had been on my mind since I got there. But there wasn't no easy way to say it, so I said, "Aunt Heather, what I need right now is money."

Counted twenty-five ticks off the wall clock. Aunt Heather got up and went to the bathroom, stayed in there about half an hour, come back and sit down. After a little, said, "You get enough to eat?"

I said I did and she said, "Claude Dee Junior, I'm pea turkey poor, you know that."

I said, "Yes, mam."

She said, "Got nothing but what's left of Edgar's war insurance, bless his sweet soul. Ain't hardly enough to keep body and soul together."

I said, "No, mam."

Counted another twenty-five ticks off the clock.

She said, "How much you talking about needing?"

I said, "Down payment on a car. Can't walk to the promised land. Enough left over for a nice suit of clothes. I figure three hundred dollars will set my feet on the road to glory."

"And mine on the road to the poor house," she said. Made a mournful sound, said, "Perish the day wherein I was born."

I said, "Book of Job, chapter three."

Later we sit on the front porch, not talking, just like olden times. The moon shimmered down through the mulberry tree and off somewheres in the night a lorn dog was barking and the air was heavy with the smell of honeysuckle.

I got to thinking how life narrows down to just one thing at a time and how you can't do nothing about what's already happened, and not a hellova lot about what's coming next. How life ain't measured out like we think in days and weeks and years, but only in just moments that come and go. And once they're gone there ain't nothing left but memories.

Like that night. Me and Aunt Heather sitting on the porch, surrounded by the sweet darkness, the cicadas singing soft in the trees. And what happened was a strange feeling welled up in my soul, a feeling lonely but peaceful too, and I thought, right now, for just this one moment anyways, I'm free and also maybe happy.

After a little Aunt Heather said something she must a thought was funny, but my mind was off somewheres else, so I said, "Yes, mam."

She said, "Claude Dee, you ain't heard a word I said."

I said, "No, mam."

She said, "Trouble with you, boy, you take yourself too serious. Always did. How come you don't never laugh?"

I said, "I don't reckon I know how."

She said, "Don't you think nothing's funny?"

I said, "Yes, mam. Damn near everything."

━━━━━━━━━━━━

Said, "Well, well, if it ain't Claude Dee Junior. Don't look like that vacation up at Pordell done you no harm."

Standing there in that baby blue polyester suit, two sizes too small, pecker-sprung and frazzled at the sleeves. Belly hanging over his belt buckle like a sack of shelled corn, face splotched with busted veins from drinking bad whiskey. A Nixon-for-President button pinned to his coat. One of them bonhomey bastards you don't need no good reason to dislike.

I said, "Gussie, I ain't here to discuss my recent penal servitude, I'm looking to buy a car."

"Come to the right honcho," he said. "What kind of a down you thinking about?"

I said, "Not no hellova lot. I ain't had time to trade in my government bonds. Twenty-five's the limit."

He give me a slant look, said, "I can't put you in no Cadillac for that."

I said, "I ain't looking for no Cadillac. All I need's something that'll take me from here to there."

He said, "And where might that be, Claude Dee?"

I said, "The land of Goshen."

He said, "Well, I ain't never been to Goshen, but I got a cream puff down here that's going to bring tears to your eyes."

Walked off down the lot, stopped at a purple 1952 Dodge. One of them batmobiles with flanged rear fenders, a little hunkered down on one side.

He said, "Christmas done come early for you, son, I bought this baby right."

I give her a casual going over, said, "Local owned."

He said, "Nope, come up from Louisiana. Natchitoches to be exact. Previous owner the Reverend Arnold Titsworth. Friend of mine down there checked her out, says she's solid as Mount Rushmont."

Rushmount.

I wrestled open the front door, checked the speedometer. Read 24,000 miles, exact. Dumb.

I said, "Who run off the mileage, you or the Reverend Titsworth?"

Pained look come on his face, said, "Wait a minute, boy, that speedometer ain't been tampered with. What you're seeing is what you're getting."

I said, "Yeah, I know, fuck your Aunt Sadie, tell them it was Marilyn Monroe."

He said, "My word's my bond, Claude Dee. Anybody'll tell you that."

I said, "Look, Gussie, might be best we just take an oaten vow not to shit each other."

Laid his hand on my shoulder, said, "Claude Dee, me and you knowed each other since before we was born. I sure as hell ain't going to screw an old buddy."

Old buddy's ass. Only socializing we ever done was back in the tenth grade when he beat hell out of me over a casual remark I made about his sister Verna.

I said, "What you got on this here relic?"

I said, "Round her off at three."

He said, "Three fifty. Twenty-five down, pay off the balance twenty-five a month."

I stood there studying the toe of my boot, waiting him out. He said, "Throw in a fifth of prime bourbon for measure."

I give him twenty-five dollars, he went and got the keys and a jug of Green Hill. *Prime bourbon.*

I started the batmobile, revved her up a time or two. Sounded like somebody throwed a handful of rivets in the manifold. Gussie stood there solemn as a hanging judge, leaned a little forward, lowered his voice, said, "Son, I'd appreciate it you didn't tell nobody what you paid for this car. I done took a shafting today, ain't something I'd want to get around."

Thought, should a put my money in fools. I'd be rich now.

Said, "I was you, Gussie, I'd do some hard praying. Good chance you done already committed the unpardonable sin."

Chapter Two

Drove over to the mill commissary, bought a can of coffee, three day old pound cake, a case of Lone Star beer. Old man Dolph Roberts, slack-jawed and bleary-eyed, give me the once over, said, "You back for good, Claude Dee?"

A screwball question, said, "No, sir, just home on a vacation."

Stopped at the iceplant, picked up fifty pounds of ice, set out for my place. Hadn't got much passed Caney Fork creek that batmobile started trailing blue smoke, told myself, next time I'm in town remind me to kick the shit out of Gussie Barnes.

Coming down the wagon trail where Larry Lee fell mortally wounded, that farm, hard in sunlight, didn't look

like nothing you'd worked your ass off to own. Parked the
Dodge in the shade of a tree, went inside. Worse than I
remembered, but no time to piss and moan. Cleaned up
the kitchen, unclogged the commode, brought a bucket of
water up from the creek and scrubbed the chickenshit off
the back porch. Went down to the barn, found a rusty weed
cutter, come back to the garden, tore out that rotted fence,
set in on them weeds. Me and that dominicker hen, me
slashing around out there like a bobcat got his balls
caught in a bear trap, her scratching and clucking, eating
grubs fast as I could turn them up.

It was getting on towards sundown when I finished up,
raked the dead weeds in a pile, set fire to them, then went
and sit on the back steps. Bone weary and sweating like
a Frisco whore at a national fuckoff, but feeling pretty
good about what I done.

About then seen that gimpy-legged bluetick hound down
by the lot gate, standing there watching me, a sad-eyed
forlorn creature without home or loved ones. Tore at my
heart. Give him a friendly whistle and a Christian name,
said, "Come over here, Elijah, I ain't going to chunk you
no more."

After a little he come a step or two, then stopped, having
learned I reckon that one sure way to get your ass knocked
off is by putting too much faith in friendly strangers. After
a little more coaxing he come on, a step at a time, rear
end hunkered down so low he left a pecker track in the
dust. Finally he got close enough for me to reach out and
scratch his ear, then we went inside and I opened a bottle
of beer and poured him some in a tin pan and we both
eat a chunk of dried pound cake. That's the way me and
him become mortal friends.

─────

Voices said, "Too hot to poot, ain't it?"

Looked up, seen Harley Biggs standing at the screen door. He come on in without being asked, helped hisself to a beer, sit down. Same old Harley, squirrely face, half a chin, mouthful of rotted teeth. Back in high school me and him used to fight every afternoon on the way home. Best friends in them days.

He said, "I heard up town you was home."

I said, "Well, you heard right."

He said, "That your car out there?"

I said, "Mine, Aunt Heather's, and the Lord's."

He took a swig of beer, looking at Elijah, said, "Got you a dog?"

I said, "Have now."

He said, "He got a name?"

I said, "Elijah."

He shook his head, said, "I ain't never heard of a dog named Elijah."

I said, "Harley, we ain't got enough time to discuss all the things you ain't never heard of."

He got us another beer and we went and sit on the back porch. A little breeze was stirring and you could hear the hornets fretful in the blackjack sprout.

After a little Harley said, "You ever find it in your heart to forgive Larry Lee?"

I said, "Nothing to forgive, Larry Lee's in the bosom of Abraham." I said anyhow it wasn't something I cared to talk about.

He said, "What do you aim to do now?"

I said, "Revival preaching."

He give me a slant look, said, "You're shitting old Harley, ain't you?"

I said, "I ain't no longer in the business of shitting people. I been called to it."

He said, "Well, you was always a talker. Where you aim to do this preaching?"

I said, "Wherever there's sinners in need."

He give me a little grin, said, "Way I hear it, revival preachers gets lots of poony."

Got a foul mind, Harley has. I said, "Goddam it, Harley, I ain't in it for the poony. This here's a spiritual matter."

He sit a minute, picking his nose, then said, "Who you got to lead singing?"

I said I hadn't give that much thought.

He said, "I can sing." I let that pass and he said, "You want to hear me?"

I said, "No."

He said, "How about What a Friend We Have in Jesus?"

I said, "Be fine, Harley."

So he stood up and croaked out three verses, pitching it two keys too high. I seen he'd even got the attention of the dominicker hen up in the garden.

He finished I sit looking off towards the creek and after a little he said, "Well, what do you think?"

I said, "You always scratch your ass when you sing?"

He said, "Chiggers. Ain't nothing I can do about that."

I said well I'd think about the singing but I thought he ought to get him some coal oil, try to get on top of them chiggers.

We sit awhile not saying nothing, then he asked me something but my mind was off somewheres else and I didn't care to have the question repeated so let it pass.

Harley said, "I reckon you want to be alone."

I said truth was I had some serious thinking I needed to do, but was anyways glad he come out.

He stood up, said, "I ain't one to hang around where I ain't wanted." I said it wasn't nothing like that and he said, "I'll be looking to hear from you." Then he went off around the house.

I said, "Say hello to your mama and them," but I reckon his feelings was hurt because he didn't say nothing and kept on a walking.

After Harley left me and Elijah went down to the creek and took a swim. Afterwards we sit on the bank and watched the day end, the sun dropping sudden behind the hills, the willows along the creek blood red in sunlight, then the blue haze settled over Butternut mountain as dusk come down. A stillness fell over everything, the on-liest sound was the slow murmur of the creek and the soft hum of insects in the trees. A sweet peace come over my soul there ain't words to explain.

Said to Elijah, "It's times like this that counts, ain't it."

Then I remembered Ada, the way her face was born to smile when something pleased her, and the way she'd sometimes tilt her head a little to one side and look at me and say just my name.

Alone is mostly good, but there's things that want sharing.

Next morning me and Elijah walked to town and I bor-rowed some tools from Tooter Roberts and went back to the farm and spent the rest of the day tearing down the intake manifold in the Dodge. Somewhere along there I got to thinking about what Aunt Heather had said, that I ought to get myself ordained to preach, but trouble with that was I wasn't on exactly intimate terms with none of the preachers in Howtown. To tell the truth I hadn't never even been in a church that I could remember. Then I thought about Brother Roscoe Grimes, a black preacher down at Grey's Landing that I used to sometimes fish the river with, back before I committed that crime of passion on Larry Lee. Thought, maybe he'd ordain me and maybe he wouldn't but I didn't have no better idea, so late that afternoon after I'd put that manifold back together me and Elijah drove out to Caddo river bottom.

Grey's Landing ain't nothing but a piss stop, maybe a hundred poor blacks working somebody else's land, clinging to hope and salvation. Church sits back in a grove of pinoaks at the edge of town, surrounded by cotton fields that near come up to the windows. Sign out front says: GREY'S LANDING BAPTIST CHURCH OF THE HOLY WITNESS. Out back a white-washed shotgun shack with a few scraggly flowers in the yard where Brother Roscoe and his wife Pearly Mae lived. Hound dog come from under the shack, barked a time or two, but him and Elijah give each other a friendly sniffing and he called off the attack.

Wasn't nobody at the house so I went ahead on, seen Brother Roscoe handpole fishing off a rickety dock down by the river bend.

Went down there, come up behind him, said, "Ain't no fish in that river, me and you caught them all a long time ago."

He stood up and shook my hand, give me a warm welcome, a scrawny little man with wispy white hair. Said, "Boy, I thought they had you locked up."

I said, "No, sir, paid my debt to society. Got time off for good behavior, warden said take up thy bed and walk."

He said, "There's another pole up at the house, I got enough bait for both of us."

I said I was obliged but I didn't have time to do no fishing, that I was there on more serious business.

He eased his minner back in the water, said, "I'm listening."

I said, "Well, Brother Roscoe, while I was locked up I took to reading the bible, first because there wasn't nothing else to read, then later because I was filled with the holy ghost. Read that bible whenever I had a spare moment, day and night, then along there somewheres it come in my mind that the Lord was calling me to preach. I fought it for awhile but the Lord prevailed against me, so soon as I can get myself ordained I'm going out among the sinners."

He didn't say nothing for a good little while, just sit there staring at his cork, then he said, "You saved, boy?"

I said, "Yes, sir. Taken Jesus Christ as my personal savior in that cell up at Pordell." He didn't say nothing to that, so I said, "I don't reckon you have to stand up in a church to be saved."

He said, "No, I don't reckon you do." Waited a little, said, "So you want me to ordain you?"

I said, "Yes, sir, I do, if your heart's easy with it."

He said, "It ain't for me to judge. Judge not lest ye be judged."

I said, "Yes, sir, Book of Matthew, seventh verse."

He give me a slant look, went back to his fishing, after a little said, "What's white folks going to say, you being ordained in a black church?"

I said, "I ain't worried none about that. Like Paul says in the Book of Galatians, there ain't no difference between Jew and Greek, free men and slaves. I figure that means blacks and whites too. I don't reckon nobody's going to argue with Paul."

He sit a little longer, stood and took in his pole, said, "I reckon you're right about this river. Fished out. I ain't caught nothing down here since last Spring." Stood there giving me a long hard look, said, "Go around spouting scripture don't mean you been called to the Lord's work."

I said, "No, sir, any fool can spout scripture."

He walked off towards the house and I went along, when we got up there he said, "Claude Dee, ordination is a serious thing. Me and you done some fishing together, had some good times. Spite of what you done it don't trouble me to call you friend, but what you're asking now puts a burden on my conscience."

I said, "I know that, Brother Roscoe. You ain't easy with it, don't do it."

He stood looking down at the ground a pretty good while, said, "I'll get two or three of my deacons together, you be here at the church tomorrow afternoon at three."

I started to offer him my hand but didn't want it to look like I was pushing our former friendship, so I said, "I'm obliged to you, Brother Roscoe. I'll try to be worthy of your trust."

He said, "Mind you, there won't be no special favors. Them deacons know the bible forwards and backwards. You'll be treated like anybody else comes up for ordination."

I said, "Yes, sir. I wouldn't want it no other way."

I was leaving, he said, "Looks like that dog of yours could use a little fattening up."

I said, "Well, he just lately come under my care. I'm working on it."

Drove home on the river road, past them cotton field shacks, warped and weather-washed. Seen now and then black kids along the road, dressed in tatters or nothing atall, bellies pooched out from eating nothing but fried taters and blackstrap molasses. Seen an old man, too wore out to work any longer in the fields, sitting in shadows on the front steps, staring off towards the river. Waiting I reckon for dark to come on so he could go to bed and dream whatever dreams was left to him.

Got me to thinking. I lived all my life in Howtown, never give no thought to how other people lived. Says somewhere in the gospel that the poor won't never go out of the land, says even though they ain't got nothing, they're rich because the Lord's on their side. Thought, I don't reckon that's much comfort to a black man that's give his whole mortal life working somebody else's fields. Who ain't got nothing, ain't never had nothing, knows he ain't got the chance of a one-legged man in a ass kicking contest of ever getting nothing.

Thought, there ought to be a sermon in there somewheres.

Thinking about that turned my mind off in another direction, which was, was I really called to preach like I'd been telling everybody, or was I just drawed to it? It ain't something I brood about, but after what's happened since then, I still ain't exactly clear on that.

━━━━━━

On the way home, went by Aunt Heather's to borrow her bible. Wasn't nobody in the house, went on to the back porch, found her sitting there pitting wild cherries, humming Mr. Frog Went A-courting.

Told her what I come for, she said, "You ain't got a bible?"

I said, "No, mam. One I read up at Pordell was state property, I ain't had time to procure one of my own."

We went inside and she got the bible, said, "Anything happened to this I reckon I'd lay down and die. It was give to me on our wedding day by your late Uncle Edgar, bless his sweet soul."

Told her about my trip out to Grey's Landing, she said, "Grey's Landing? That's a black church."

I said, "Yes, mam, it's all the same to me, black or white." Tried a little joke, said, "Like I told them up at Pordell, we're all in this together."

She said, "That's not funny, Claude Dee."

I said, "Well, didn't nobody up at Pordell think so either."

She said, "I reckon you're hungry?"

I said I was, said me and Elijah hadn't ate nothing since the day before.

She said, "Elijah?"

I said, "Yes, mam, that's my dog. He's waiting out in the car."

She rolled her eyes up, said, "Merciful Redeemer, just what you need, a mangy hound to look after."

I said, "Way that works, we look after each other."

I went and got Elijah and she fixed us a field hand supper and later we all sit awhile on the porch, not talking much.

I got up to go, she said, "You and Elijah are welcome to stay the night here, you're amind to."

I said, "I think we best get on back to the farm, I need to do some brushing up on Deuteronomy."

She give a little sigh, said, "I hope you ain't fixing to bring down more shame on me, Claude Dee."

Give her a kiss on the cheek, said, "Don't you worry none about that, Aunt Heather, I'm on the Lord's team now."

She said, "Well, it ain't the first time he's picked a loser."

━━━━━━━━━━━━━

Next day I drove out to Grey's Landing under heavy skies. Thunder rumbling above the peaks of Butternut mountain, jagged streaks of lightening along the river, heavy overcast not much higher than the treetops. Got darker and darker, then about Pooley's creek the skies let loose and the rain come down like a cow pissing on a flat rock.

Wondered was the Lord sending me a sign.

Brother Roscoe and his two deacons was waiting for me at the church. We went inside and there was a long table down by the pulpit with three chairs on one side and a chair for me on the other.

Brother Roscoe first introduced me to the deacons, Brother Williams, a skinny little man with owl eyes, carrying three or four books, and Brother Samuels, who must a weighed three hundred pounds, wearing overalls a white shirt and necktie.

We sit down and Brother Roscoe told Brother Williams to lead it off.

Brother Williams kind of smiled, nodded, said, "Mr. Moran, we might just start off with a question of a theological nature. How do you stand on the subject of post-millennialism versus pre-millennialism?"

Thought, Lordamighty.

Said, "Well, sir, to tell the truth seems like I run hot and cold on that. Seems like one day I'll be pre, next day maybe I'm post."

Brother Williams sit there a minute, looking down at a pencil he'd been fiddling with. Seen right away I wasn't shitting nobody.

But Brother Williams was kindly about it, which I appreciated, said, "Well, there's some strong bible scholars still arguing that one. Let's move on to something else. How do you feel about the trinity?"

I said, "Yes, sir, you mean the father, son, and holy ghost?" He nodded, I said, "Well, I'm for it. The way I see it, if there wasn't no father and son there probably wouldn't be no christianity. I do have a little trouble with the holy ghost but nothing serious. That's one of them deep things I take on faith."

He said, "Then you do believe in the virgin birth?"

I said, "Yes, sir, I do." Didn't want my answer to sound too simple, so threw in something I made up. Said, "I think McGiffert explained that to my satisfaction."

Brother Williams glance over at Brother Roscoe, said, "Which McGiffert is that?"

Nothing to do but bluff her through. Said, "Thomas Abercrombie McGiffert. Wrote the Latter Day Commentaries on the New Testament. Read him while I was up at Pordell prison."

Seemed like about a minute passed without nobody saying nothing. I could hear the rain beating on the roof and the wind rattling one of the windows in the back of the church.

Finally, Brother Roscoe said, "Do you have a question, Brother Samuels?"

Brother Samuels cleared his throat a time or two, said, "Mr. Moran, we all know the bible is sometimes a puzzle, us poor mortals find in it many twists and turns, yea, we sometimes falter, looking through a glass darkly, but the way of salvation is straight as the flight of an arrow, for God so loved the world that he gave his only begotten son, that whosoever believes in him shall have eternal life. Is that what you believe, Mr. Moran?"

I said, "Ever mortal word of it."

He said, "For the son of man is not come to destroy men's lives but to save them. Neither is there salvation in any other, for there is none other name under heaven given among men whereby we might be saved. Who is a liar but he that denieth that Jesus is the Christ? He is antichrist that denieth the father and the son."

He stopped and sit looking at me, but I didn't hear no question in there, so I said, "amen."

He went off on another short sermon about salvation, mostly from Psalms, but there wasn't no question asked so when he finished I said, "Brother Samuels, I just want to say I ain't never heard nobody quote scripture the way you do, man knows his bible like you ought to be a preacher hisself."

He give me a little nod, said to Brother Roscoe, "No more questions."

I felt some better about my chances, but not for long. Brother Williams come at me again, wanting to know how I felt about substitutionary atonement and the doctrine of plenary inspiration and something about the devil called the ransom theory. Might as well a asked me why a farting horse never tires.

I was trying to dog it and not getting nowhere when Brother Roscoe come to my rescue, said, "I think we've pretty well covered the scripture, Mr. Moran. Maybe you'd like to tell us in your own words what you feel is your basic mission as a preacher."

I'd give that some thought. Said, yes, sir, I would, that I appreciated the chance. Said mainly I wanted to preach to everyday people going about their everyday lives, black and white, old and young, rich and poor, but mostly poor. Said I wanted to preach the religion of joy and forgiveness, that it seemed like the bible was mostly talking about what people couldn't do, you couldn't steal, you couldn't covet another man's woman, you couldn't this and couldn't that. Said I wanted to preach about what people could do, the gospel of you can do it. Remembered something I read in that greatest books ever wrote course, said, I wanted people to know theirself, to search their own souls and find the peace that passeth all understanding, that I wanted to reach out to them that couldn't help their own selves. Got a little carried away, started quoting scripture, said, but as for me when they was sick, my clothing was sackcloth, I humbled my soul with fasting and my prayer returned unto mine own bosom, thus speaketh the Lord of hosts, saying, execute true judgment and show mercy and compassion to every man, rejoice with them that rejoice and weep with them that weep.

Went on like that a little, then wrapped her up. Said, "I reckon it all comes down to the gospel of love, for he that loveth not knoweth not God. I'd say that one line of scripture pretty well sums up the abiding gospel of Claude Dee Moran Junior."

For about a minute nobody said nothing, Brother Williams was writing something on a piece of paper, then Brother Roscoe said, "Mr. Moran, I'll just ask you to step outside for a few minutes, we'll call you back in when we've reached a decision."

I went out front and sit on the steps and waited, figuring I'd pretty much blowed my chances of being ordained. Then I remembered something Aunt Heather used to tell me when I was a kid, come to her fretting about something. She'd say, "Boy, don't worry about nothing that can't kill you." Lots she taught me.

The rain had passed through and off to the west the sky was clearing. Ain't nothing more interesting than watching clouds after a rain storm, the way they break up and come together again, pushed along by the wind. I'd say I'm pretty near a expert on clouds.

After about fifteen minutes Brother Roscoe come to the door and called me back inside. I went and sit down and Brother Roscoe said, "Claude Dee, let me say right off that the committee views your future ministry with some misgiving." Thought, here it is, the shit's done hit the fan. Brother Roscoe went ahead, said, "You been studying your bible, we got no concern about that, but Brother Williams has some serious doubts about your theology. However, we know theology ain't preaching and preaching ain't theology. I will say we was impressed with your final statement and the sincerity of your faith. Mainly on the strength of that, it is our decision that on this day you be duly ordained a minister of the Baptist faith."

We all stood up and shook hands and I said, "I want to thank you gentlemen for a fair trial." Didn't quite come out right but I meant it.

Brother Williams and Brother Samuels left and Brother Roscoe went to a room off to one side and after a little brought back a certificate which said that I, Claude Dee Moran Junior, was ordained in the Church of the Holy Witness to preach the gospel of Jesus Christ.

I thanked him again, he told me to let him know when I was ready to go fishing, then I got in my car and lit out for home, feeling I admit pretty good.

Time I got back to the farm the sky was clear and the sun beat down unmerciful, raising heat waves from the damp fields. I drove up behind the house, Elijah come out to meet me, kind of hunkering down like he always did. I said, "Stand up there, boy, you're looking at the Reverend Claude Dee Moran Junior." Seen then the grey feather the corner of his mouth, thought, Godamighty, he's done dispatched that dominicker, which he done. Found what was left of her under the corner of the well porch, started to grab up something and beat the peewadden out of Elijah, then thought again. Thought, it's all the same, the law of the jungle, the law of the world, the weak and the strong. Sad to say.

Give Elijah a hard talking to, my first sermon I reckon you could say, then went and got us a beer and we sit on the porch and finished off that pound cake.

Had another beer and a weariness come over me from my day's labors, so I stretched out and closed my eyes. Was about half asleep when I got to thinking about what used to be.

Back after me and Ada had bought the farm I'd come in at noon, woreout from grubbing blackjacks or digging stumps, and I'd stretch out on the back porch till Ada got dinner ready. She'd come to the door and stand there looking at me, then she'd laugh and go back inside without saying nothing, and a minute later I'd hear her in the kitchen singing that song. Went like this, Lazy bones, sleeping in the sun, how you going to get your day's work done, never get your day's work done, sleeping in the noonday sun.

Had a pure voice, Ada did, sweet as a meadowlark calling the morning to life. Good times them.

Fell asleep, had one of them dreams about Ada, not the first time. Woke me up. Went down and jumped in the creek. Clothes and all.

Chapter Three

Sitting on the back porch working on my revival budget, looked up seen Harley coming around the corner of the house.

He said, "I been waiting for you to call."

I said, "Ain't got my phone hooked up yet."

He said, "You got time to talk?"

I said, "Just give me a few minutes, Harley, I'm doing a little financial figuring."

He sit down on the steps, pulled a magazine out of his pocket and started reading it. One of them porno things. Now and then he'd make a strange sound, somewheres between a giggle and a grunt, after a little, looked up, said, "What's oral sex?"

I said, "That's when you fuck and talk at the same time."

He said, "I don't understand that. What is they to talk about?"

Ain't but one Harley.

I said, "In your case, Harley, I'd say not no hellova lot."

He give me a look, said, "You guying me?"

I said, "Yeah, I reckon I am."

Trouble with my budget was I didn't have enough money. I'd went up to town Saturday, got to asking around, run into A. L. Allen, he told me about a man over at Cordell had a big tent he wanted to sell. Drove over there, talked to a man name Pruitt. Had a tent all right, said he bought it from some defunct Holy Rollers, only thing, he wanted two hundred dollars for it. Figured I could get him down to a hundred and fifty, but that still meant I'd have to borrow more money from Aunt Heather. Or somebody else.

Said, "Harley, you got any money?" He said, "Four dollars and something, owe two of that to Fidge Hawkins, money I lost in a kelly pool game."

I said, "You got anything we might sell, our cash flow is down to a drip."

He said, "Pickup truck. Don't run though, stripped the rear end out of it hauling hay last summer."

I said, "We can put another rear end in it, ain't nothing else wrong."

Harley said, "Nothing I know of. Been sitting there a year."

Had a beer then went over to Harley's house, you could call it that, a shotgun shack half growed over with weeds. The truck sit out in the back lot, a 1958 Ford, a sorry sight, paint peeling, tires pretty near rotted off. Still, it was something.

I went up town, reborrowed Tooter's tools, went out to Biglow's Used Auto Parts, found some rear end gearing I figured would work, went back out to Harley's and set in on that pickup. Put him to cutting back weeds and scraping paint, I dropped the rear end, started setting them gears in. Hot work. Been at it awhile, Harley said, "What worries me, what if we do all this work, then can't make no money in the revival business."

I said, "Harley, don't worry about nothing that can't kill you."

He said, "You don't worry about nothing, do you?"

I said, "Damn near everything."

He said, "What's something you worry about?"

I said, "Getting bit by a rabid squirrel."

He grinned, said, "You're shitting old Harley again, ain't you?"

Worked till dark, most of the next day, on that pickup. I finally got the rear end put back together, Harley give her a new paint job. Turdmuckle yellow. We jump started her off my battery, drove up to Tooter's garage, tuned up the motor, put on four new used tires, stuck a For Sale sign on the windshield, parked her out front, then went over to the Eagle cafe for a beer and waited.

Sitting there jiving with Big Tits Brenda, couldn't a been more than half a hour later, this tall skinny jake come in. Come over to where we was sitting, said, "You Claude Dee Moran?"

I said, "Yes, sir. Junior."

He said, "That your pickup with the For Sale sign on it?"

I said it was, he said, "What you asking for it?"

Said, "I'm giving it away."

He said, "Giving it away?"

I said, "Same as. It's a giveaway at five hundred." Left myself some swapping space, done figured I'd let her go for three.

He just stood there looking down at the floor. I said, "Wouldn't sell it atall I didn't need some quick money." He still didn't look up or say nothing. I said, "I got a sick mama, has to have a spinal operation."

He shook his head, said, "Five's too rich for my blood."

I said, "How rich a blood you got?"

He said, "I might go high as four, she drives out clean."

I said, "You talking cash money?"

He said, "That's what I'm talking."

I said, "Let's go kick her in the ass."

Went back over to Tooter's, he give the motor a going over, then we got in and took a test run. Got out on the highway he eased her up around fifty-five, me sitting there holding my breath and praying them rear end gears didn't fly apart.

Back at Tooter's garage he said, "I'll take it." Counted me out twenty double sawbucks and drove off, never even told me his name.

Same afternoon me and Harley drove over to Cordell and looked up Mr. Pruitt. Me and him sit astraddle the fence like two Yell county mule traders, a hard man to do business with, thin-lipped and mean-eyed, giving ground a dime at a time. Tobacco chewer, never spoke a sentence more than ten words.

Sun going down. I said, "You understand I'm a preacher."

Sit there looking off towards the hills, said, "Don't mean nothing. Preacher's dicks get hard same as mine."

Another half hour, dusk coming on, nothing moving. Seen we'd hit bedrock, settled for a hundred eighty-four dollars and fifty cents.

Me and Harley lashed the tent on top of the batmobile, set out for home.

Soon as we got clear of Pruitt's drive, Harley said, "Godamighty, we're on our way, ain't we?"

I said, "Somewheres."

We got back to my place, I broke out that bottle of rat poison Gussie give me, me and Harley sit on the back porch and drunk a few toasts. Drunk to me being ordained, drunk to the sale of Harley's pickup, drunk to the purchase of a tent, drunk to our future success on the revival trail. Run out of occasions, so we drunk to Elijah, Big Tits Brenda, Ada, Aunt Heather, Larry Lee, Harley's dead mama. Run out of people, so we drunk to fire, wind, plagues, I don't remember what all. Fact is, I don't remember much of the rest of that day or night. Next thing I knew it was around ten the next morning. Sit up feeling like I'd come out second best in a stomping match. Seen Harley piled up on the floor, kicked him awake, he blinked twice, said, "Where we at?"

Said, "Thou, which art exaulted unto heaven, shalt be brought down to hell. Book of Matthew."

———————————

Me and Harley was sitting in the Eagle cafe having a beer, got to talking about where we was going to hold our first revival.

I said, "We need a town not too big, got a high ratio of unsaved sinners."

Harley said, "That there'd be your democrats."

I said, "You telling me there's more unsaved democrats than they is republicans?"

He said, "It's a known fact."

I said, "Wonder why that is?"

He said, "I don't know, it just is. Known fact that democrats drink more, commit more adultery, raise more hell."

I didn't put much faith in that theory but didn't have no better one, so said, "How we going to know if a town has more democrats than republicans?"

He said, "Go to the courthouse, look at your registration lists."

I said, "Reckon they'll let us do that?"

He said, "Don't, we'll take them to court. That there's your public domain."

Times, Harley wasn't as dumb as he looked. Quite.

So that's what we done. Next two days we drove all over Pontotoc county checking registration lists. Turned out the place we was looking for was Caledonia, a town twenty-five miles to the north, on the Saline river. Population 1247, four hundred and twenty-three registered to vote, all but six democrats.

Cruised around awhile looking the town over, one long street, few stores, couple of hog waller beer joints. Houses on the back streets mostly rundown, yards overgrowed, couple of bare-ass kids playing in the dust out back of the schoolhouse.

Harley said, "Well, what do you think?"

Said, "If there be among you the poor, thou shalt not harden thy heart nor shut thine hand from thy poor brethren."

Harley said, "That more of the gospel?"

Said, "Book of Job, twelfth chapter." Guessed on that one, but what the hell did Harley know. As has been said many a time, you don't always know exactly what you're talking about, best you're talking to people don't know nothing atall.

Drove back to the upper end of town, seen two old cooters sitting on a bench in front of the Farmer's Bank, eased over there, got out, stuck out my hand, said, "The Reverend Claude Dee Moran Junior." Didn't shake my hand or say nothing, just sit there looking at me, sullen-eyed old farts.

Said, "I'll be bringing my revival team in here next week, what I need is a place to set up my tent, preferable not too far from town."

They sit a little thinking it over, then one with the turkey neck said, "Last tent revival come in here, four or five years ago, set up out on Dolph Dickerson's farm."

Give me directions how to get there, me and Harley drove out that way. Farm about two miles from town,

two-story house back aways off the road, woodlands on the
right, a cutover meadow off to the left. We got out of the
car, thought I seen a woman looking out the upstairs window, could a been wrong, just there and gone. Anyhow, I
couldn't rouse nobody knocking at the front door, so me and
Harley walked around back. Seen a man down at the barn
lot, setting in fence posts. Went down there, told him who
I was, said my business was revival preaching. He kept
pounding away with that post hole digger, didn't give me
even a look. Tall fellar, sunken eyed and bushy browed.

I said, "Looks like you could use some help." Bam bam.
Might as well a been talking to one of them posts he was
setting in. Said, "Man up town told me you'd maybe let
me put my tent in your meadow." Still didn't say nothing,
close as a bastard boy at a family reunion. Said, "You are
Mr. Dickerson, ain't you?"

Hit her another lick or two, stepped back, took a ban-
dana out of his pocket and wiped his face, then give me
a long steady look. Said, "What church you with?"

Said, "I ain't with no church at the moment. I'm what
they call a minister of the Free Apostolic Movement."
Made that up but couldn't think of nothing else to say.

Dickerson spit a squirt of tobacco juice at the post hole,
stood there studying the toe of his boot.

I said, "Mr. Dickerson, my associate will be glad to spell
you on that digger." Said, "Harley, worry that hole along
while me and Mr. Dickerson do a little parleying."

Harley said, "Me?"

I said, "Harley."

Dickerson handed him the digger, me and him went
over and hunkered kown in the breezeway of his barn.
Tough as a dried possum prick, Dickerson was, said I could
set my tent up in his meadow for five dollars a night.
Offered him two, said it was the Lord's work. Said that
didn't mean nothing to him, it was still five dollars a night.

I said, "Mr. Dickerson, I'm going to ask you to do something that could well change the course of your life. I'm going to ask you to kneel with me right here, let me pray with you."

Dickerson said, "I ain't a praying man."

I said, "Therefore I say unto you, what things soever ye desire, when ye pray, believe that ye receive them and they shall be yours. Book of Mark."

Dickerson said, "Horseshit."

Seen I was dealing with a hardened heart, offered him three dollars, said that was my top price. Settled for four.

Paid him three days in advance, me and Harley drove back to town. Went to the drugstore, bought some poster boards and one of them magic markers, made four signs that said BIG TENT REVIVAL, DOLPH DICKERSON'S FARM, BEGINS SUNDAY NIGHT 7:00 O'CLOCK, FIRST SERMON "IS FORNICATION A SIN?"—THE REVEREND CLAUDE DEE MORAN JUNIOR PREACHING, BROTHER HARLEY BIGGS SONGMASTER. It was Harley thought of that songmaster.

Made four more signs, said WANTED, VOLUNTEERS, BOYS AND GIRLS TO HELP SET UP A REVIVAL TENT, REPORT TO DOLPH DICKERSON'S FARM SUNDAY, 12:30—"THE SLEEP OF A LABORING MAN IS SWEET, WHETHER HE EAT LITTLE OR MUCH," BOOK OF ECCLESIASTES.

Put the signs up in store windows around town, lit out for home. Stopped in Hardecke, bought a case of Lone Star to stave off a heat stroke, hadn't drove far Harley said, "It don't bother you none, you a preacher, drinking beer?"

Said, "Don't bother me atall. Bible ain't against drinking. Famous miracle's the one where Jesus was at a party when they run out of wine. Somebody brought in a bucket of water and he waved his hand over it, next thing you know they had a bucket of wine."

Harley said, "How'd he do that?"

I said, "I don't know, he just done it."

Harley said, "Don't make sense, does it?"

I said, "Damnit, Harley, it ain't supposed to make sense. We're talking here about a miracle."

Drove a little on, Harley said, "You telling me Jesus was a drinker?"

Trouble with talking to Harley, he don't know when to let go.

I said, "I don't know Harley. I reckon he'd have a glass of wine, maybe a can of beer now and then."

Harley said, "What kind of party was it?"

I said, "A wedding party, Harley. In the land of Cana."

Drove a little on, Harley said, "How many people was there?"

Thought, shit, Harley. Said, "Twenty-six, counting Jesus."

Harley said, "I don't know. It don't make sense to me."

Driving back to Howtown it come to me that I didn't know nothing about how to run a church service, so I said, "Harley, you ever go to church?"

He said, "Went now and then before mama died."

I said, "How exactly do we go about holding a service?"

He said, "Nothing to it. You start with a short prayer. Then I lead the congregation in a song. You pray again. After that I sing a solo. You read the scripture, what it is you're going to preach about. I sing another solo. Then you preach a sermon. After that somebody takes up collection while I'm singing another solo. Then we all sing a invitation hymn, that's when them that wants to come down front. Some taking Jesus as their personal savior, some rededicating their lives, some just farting around, wanting to be seen. All that time you'll be up there telling them how if they ain't saved they'll go to hell, and how if they don't get saved right then they'll probably drop dead and won't get no other chance, You know. more or less scaring the shit out of them. We see there ain't nobody else coming down, you pray and we go home. Nothing to it."

Except for all them solos Harley was going to sing, it sounded fine.

It was late afternoon we got back to his house. I asked him if had fitten clothes for a songmaster, said he had a suit and shirt but didn't have no necktie. Told him I'd take care of that, he got out and walked off.

Heard him say, "I don't drink much wine myself."

Everybody ought to know a Harley.

On the way home drove by Aunt Heather's, found her in the garden out back bugging tomato vines. She never seen me come up, so I sit awhile on the steps watching her, little piss ant of a woman, her face covered by a blue bonnet, hunkered down looking for them lady bugs. Made my heart ache thinking about all she'd done for me, looking after me through good times and bad, back when I wasn't no more than a addle-headed kid, nothing on my mind but popping beer cans and trying now and again to dick some wayward female.

Time I shot down Larry Lee, come to town, turned myself in to Otis Birdsong, somebody went and told her what happened. She come down to the jail, wasn't an hour after I got there, sit with me way into the night. Not saying nothing, wasn't nothing to say, just sitting there a sad sweet look on her face, me wanting to tell her how much it meant, her being there, but not knowing how.

My Aunt Heather. Wasn't for her, ain't no telling how I'd a turned out.

She finished out the row, come back to the house, seen me sitting there, said, "Like always, see you got here after the work was done."

I said, "Got to missing you, come to see if you was all right."

She said, "Fiddle."

Told her about selling Harley's truck and buying the tent, and how me and Harley was going to open our revival business Sunday night over at Caledonia.

She said, "Harley? How come you're taking him?"

I said, "Mostly to help set up the tent. Also he'll be leading my singing."

She looked to the heavens, said, "The wise man's eyes are in his head, but the fool walketh in darkness."

Couldn't come up with that one, said, "Yes, mam, truth is though if we hadn't a sold Harley's truck . . ."

She said, "Ecclesiastes, chapter two."

We sit awhile longer, waiting out the darkness. It come sudden to mind I still hadn't bought no proper attire for my preaching debut, and didn't have no big lot of money to buy none with.

Said, "I don't reckon you'd still have none of Uncle Edgar's clothes around."

She said, "You ain't bought no clothes yet?"

I said, "Got nothing but what's covering my woreout body."

Shook her head, said, "Claude Dee, Claude Dee, Claude Dee."

Took me to the little storeroom in the back of the house, said, "They was some things in here, the rat's ain't got them. I ain't opened this door in ten years."

Seen right away Uncle Edgar wasn't no Bo Brumfield. Found a couple of moldy shirts, three greasy ties, a scruffy pinchback suit with a button up fly. Coat fit me a little quick, britches two inches too short, still, like screwing a woman that ain't interested, it beats nothing atall.

I was ready to leave, Aunt Heather give me a sack of food she'd put together, walked me out to the car. We stood a minute under the mulberry tree sharing something that didn't need saying.

Finally I said, "You want to go to that meeting at Caledonia, I'll drive back over here and get you."

She said, "Never mind, I ain't had no recent quarrel with the Lord."

Just joshing I said, "Well, I'll pray for you."

She said, "Pray for your ownself and try to get in a word or two for Harley Biggs."

Got back to my place around eight, found Elijah waiting for me. We went in the kitchen and lit the lamp, hadn't had no time or money to hook up electricity. Poured us a beer, went out to the back porch, sit awhile listening to the sweet sounds of darkness.

Elijah finished off his beer, come over and flopped down against me, wanting I reckon like all of us something to comfort the soul.

Got to thinking about the revival over at Caledonia, how maybe they'd be a tent full of people there, all looking to me for salvation, felt a little hitch in my belly.

Said to Elijah, "I'd just as soon you didn't say nothing about it, but the Reverend Claude Dee Moran Junior is running a little scared."

Chapter Four

Picked up Harley Sunday morning. Wearing that sheeny wash-and-wear suit, shirt collar buttoned tight at the neck, hair slicked down with brillantine. Looked like he'd fell in a stock pond and drowned.

Said, "How do I look?"

I said, "Different, Harley." Let it go at that. Truth was, I didn't look like no fashion model myself.

We loaded the tent on the car, set out for Caledonia. Got to Dickerson's meadow by mid-morning. Hot as the hinges of hell. Found a level spot atop a long sloping hill running up to a grove of persimmon trees. Still three hours before our volunteers was due.

I said, "Reckon we ought to start ahead putting up the tent?"

Harley said, "Ain't a two man job, all them poles and struts. Me and you try to do it ourselves, we're just going to fuck her up."

Harley.

I said, "Harley, these kids come out to help us set up, other people we run into on the revival trail, I'd appreciate it you didn't use that kind of language."

He said, "What kind of language?"

I said, "Fuck her up, things like that."

He said, "I don't see nothing wrong with it."

I said, "I know you don't, Harley. That's what troubles me."

He give me a look, walked off up the slope, sit down under a persimmon tree. Seen I'd hurt his feelings, but figured goddam it the line had to be drawed somewheres.

Give him a few minutes to cool off, went up there and sit down. Waited him out.

After a little he said, "You know what we ain't got, don't you?"

I said, "What ain't we got, Harley?"

He said, "We ain't got no benches for them people to sit on."

I said, "Well, there ain't nothing we can do about that now. I'll think of something when the time comes. In the world ye shall have tribulation, but be of good cheer."

Sit a minute, Harley said, "Something else we ain't got's no water."

I said, "I reckon we'd a forgot our heads they wasn't hooked to our shoulders."

Told him to stay there, case some of our volunteers come early, went down to the house to ask Mr. Dickerson for the loan of a bucket and the use of his well.

Didn't appear to be nobody at home, shades all drawed, Dickerson's pickup gone. Went around to the well porch, knocked and waited, about ready to leave when the door opened.

Girl standing there, maybe eighteen, nineteen, not no raving beauty but something about her right away got your attention. One of them juicy women, dark eyes and a pouty mouth. Didn't say nothing, just stood there looking at me.

I said, "Is Mr. Dickerson around?"

She said, "No."

I said, "I don't reckon you know when he'll be back?"

She said, "No. He don't tell me nothing."

Said, "I take it you're Mr. Dickerson's daughter."

She said, "I'm Mrs. Dickerson."

Thought, Lordamighty, one of them child wives.

Said, "Well, I'm pleased to meet you. I'm the Reverend Claude Dee Moran Junior.

She said, "Mr. Dickerson's a right smart older than I am."

I said, "Yes, mam, I can see that." Them black eyes had me in a dead lock, causing some minor confusion. Said, "I was wondering could I borrow a bucket and some water, gets hot working out in that sun."

She went inside, come back in a minute with a pound lard can, said, "This ain't much bucket, but I reckon you can come back for more."

I said, "Yes, mam, that'll be fine."

I unhooked the well rope and drew a bucket of water, her all the time standing at my back watching.

Heard her say, "You married?"

Said, "Not exactly."

She said, "What does that mean?"

Said, "Means I got a wife but don't know where the hell she's at." Filled the lard can, said, "Well, I thank you, mam."

I was walking off, she said, "Gets lonely out here."

That brung me around, said, "Mam?"

She said, "You ever lonely?"

I said, "Damn near always." Didn't like the way that come out, said, "Everybody's lonely one time or another, that's one of them crosses we all have to bear." Looked her straight in the eye, said, "Loneliness comes over me, I turn to the scriptures. Come to me ye who are lonely and heavy laden and I'll give ye rest."

She said, "I'm coming to hear you preach. Seen your sign in the drugstore window. You're preaching tonight on fornication, ain't you?" Said I was, she said, "I reckon you think it's a mortal sin."

I said, "There ain't no yes or no answer to that. Depends on the situation, what preachers call fornicative revelation. I'll be clearing that up tonight."

She said, "I was twelve years old, I taken the Lord as my savior." She looked off toward the fields, didn't say nothing for a little, then said, "Only thing, I lately been having these wicked thoughts."

I said, "Yes, mam, what kind of thoughts?"

She give me a shy smile, said, "You know."

Felt a twitch in my groin, seemed like my britches was getting tighter, said, "Might be we ought to step inside out of this heat, let me do some counseling with you."

Hadn't no more than said that when I heard the pickup coming. Minute later Mr. Dickerson come by, seen us standing there, slowed up a little.

I held up the lard can, yelled out, "Come to borrow some drinking water!"

He give me a sour look, drove on to the barn lot.

Mrs. Dickerson said, "You ain't likely to save that one, he's done hardened his heart."

Went up the slope to where Harley was waiting, never looked back, come away with nothing but a lard can full of water and a slight case of stone ache.

Come one o'clock we still hadn't seen no volunteers. Thought, could a been somebody took them signs out of the store windows. Next thought, could be they ain't no kids in Caledonia wants to work their asses off in the vineyards of the Lord.

Harley had done fell asleep, stretched out there with a pained look on his face, a dribble of spit running out the corner of his mouth.

I poked him awake, took a little doing, Harley's a deep sleeper, he sit a minute scratching his ass, said, "What's happening?"

I said, "Looks like we ain't going to get no volunteers, I'm going to drive into town, see can I hire us a couple of strong backed boys."

He said, "No need to do that, don't nobody come, we'll put her up ourselves."

I said, "Harley, some day I kick the shit out of you, remember it was you drove me to it."

Looked though like we wasn't going to get no help so we laid out the tent flat on the ground, the front flap pointing towards the persimmon grove, started setting in tent poles.

Been working maybe half an hour, looked up seen our first and only volunteer coming up the slope. One of them boyish little girls, red-haired and freckle-faced, maybe twelve, thirteen years old.

Minute later she come walking up, said, "You the preacher looking for somebody to help in your revival?"

I said, "Yes, mam, the Reverend Claude Dee Moran Junior. What might your name be?"

She said, "Henry."

I said, "Well, I'm mighty pleased to have you join us, Henry. This here's my associate, Harley Biggs."

She give him a nod. Harley looked at me, said, "Little pisser like that ain't going to be no big help."

I said, "Harley."

Henry said, "I'm stronger than I look. I can whip J.D." Cut her eyes over at Harley, said, "You ain't no bigger than a popcorn fart yourself."

Changing the subject, I said, "You been saved, Henry?"

She said, "Ain't been saved, ain't looking to be. My mama sent me out here. She's a born again christian, mean as a sow in heat. Ain't drawed a sober breath since she give her life to Jesus. Figures she'll buy her way into heaven farming me out to jakeleg preachers looking for free hired help. Last summer me and Mr. Pooley painted the Baptist church."

Trying I reckon to sound like a proper preacher, I said, "Honor thy father and mother that thy days may be long in the land."

Henry said, "Cram it."

Turned out she could outwork me and Harley put together, never seen nothing like it, hit the ground running and never let up.

We got the tent in the place about the middle of the afternoon, looked nice sitting there above the slope, the persimmon trees gold in sunlight.

Said to Henry, "Me and Brother Biggs got to find us a creek, clean ourselves up a little. I thank you for helping us out. Tell your mama I thank her too."

She said, "You and Brother Biggs ain't no dirtier than I am. There's a creek over the rise, I'll show you where it's at."

She went off around the persimmon grove, me and Harley come along a little behind.

Harley said, "It ain't going to look right, us bathing with a little old girl."

I said, "Harley, we ain't going to bathe with no little girl."

Creek run along the backside of the meadow, meandering away through the willow trees. We got down there, I said, "Henry, best you find you a spot on down the creek aways, take your time, me and Brother Biggs will wait for you here."

She was done shucking her clothes off, come out of that shirt and them overalls like a snake shedding skin. Said, "Go find your own damn spot," standing there naked as a plucked chicken, took a flying start, landed slap on her belly in the middle of that creek.

Harley said, "She's a something, ain't she?"

Me and Harley went on down the creek aways, when we come back up there found Henry gone. Waited a little, then went back up to the tent. There she sit, eating persimmons.

I said, "I thought you'd gone home."

She said, "I ain't going home."

I said, "Where you going?"

She said, "Wherever you go."

I said, "No, you ain't. I don't need no little piss ant of a girl following me around."

She said, "And I don't need no shitass of a preacher telling me what I can't do. I reckon that's something we'll both have to get used to, cause the way I see it me and you are stuck with each other."

I said, "Don't push too hard on me, Henry, I got my breaking point."

She said, "I don't push lessen I'm pushed first, it comes to that, I got a breaking point my ownself."

Around six-thirty, still two good hours of daylight left, Henry went down to the main road to direct people where to park. Harley was inside the tent practicing some hymns he aimed to sing later. Told him earlier we didn't have no song books to pass out, he said it didn't make no difference, said he'd just throw in another solo or two.

Stood at the tent flap a little listening to him, thought between Harley and Henry the Lord had give me a mighty burden to bear.

I took Aunt Heather's bible, went up in the persimmon grove, trying to get it straight in my mind what I was going to say when I got up in front of all them people. Trouble was, I couldn't find nothing in the scriptures that exactly backed up my theory of fornicative revelation. Finally hit on the book of Solomon, writing down just them parts that fit in with the sermon I'd been thinking about.

Funny thing, I'd read Solomon up at Pordell, but reading it again, alone up there in that persimmon grove, a feeling come over me hard to explain. Got to thinking about Ada, that part where it talks about them lovers going forth into the fields, vines budding everywhere, all the flowers in bloom. Says, There I will give you my love.

Back before Ada profaned our sacred vows, I'd sometimes come home late from work at the plant, dead beat from heaving them blocks of ice around all day, Ada would be sitting on the back steps waiting for me, that sly look in her eyes. We'd go down to the creek, take off our clothes, swim awhile under the willows, then lay on the bank and talk till we couldn't stand it no longer, coming together like that stag and gazelle in the book of Solomon. A fierce lover, Ada was, leaving me with nothing but a heart full of love and a soul full of sweet memories.

Told myself I wasn't going to think no more about that bitter day I come in from squirrel hunting and sent Larry Lee to his maker. Brooding about the bad times don't grieve nobody but yourself. Remember only what saves you from perdition, them sweet moments that gives you the hope to keep on living.

Thought maybe somewheres along the way I'd preach a sermon on that.

About ten minutes till seven went back down to the tent, seen there wasn't but one car and a pickup truck parked in the meadow.

Harley and Henry met me at the tent flap, Harley said "Looks like she's going to be a little thin tonight, ain't but five people in there."

I said, "Where one or more is gathered together in my name."

Told Henry to get a tin plate I'd left in the car, that she'd take up the collection when it was called for, me and Harley went on in.

Two canvas folding chairs up front we'd brought along, them five hardy souls standing a little off to one side. A man, his woman, a tow-headed kid five or six years old. A runny-eyed old cooter looked like a buzzard wearing spectacles. Mrs. Dickerson, dressed I seen in one of them slightly plunging necklines.

I said, "As you folks can see, we ain't got no benches or chairs to sit on, and they's a good reason for that. This here's one of them old fashion bible revivals, like when Jesus preached to the multitudes, so just find yourselves a comfortable spot on the grass and we'll get the meeting started."

Me and Harley sit in the folding chairs, waiting for them to get settled, then I stood up and opened with a prayer. Wasn't nothing much, just blessing them that come and thanking the Lord for his kindness and bounty, then I sit down.

Harley got up to sing his first solo, I seen Mrs. Dickerson was sitting down pretty close, her leg folded up under her in such a way as to display about eight inches of bare thigh. Thought, that there woman's ready for a flogging. Next thought, shit, boy, you got to shun them unclean thoughts, purify thy spirit lest ye be struck dumb by the almighty wrath of the Lord. Told myself to just point my eyes somewheres else, had a week to see which direction Mrs. Dickerson was likely to jump. All things in the fullness of time.

Harley said we had a order of songbooks coming out of Chicago but they hadn't yet arrived which was why he was going to sing some special numbers. Said any of them knew the song, feel free to join in. Then he cut loose on "Rescue The Perishing", as usual pitching her about two keys too high. Standing there his head throwed back, veins in his neck looked like they was about to pop. Sounded like a constipated screech owl.

Seen that kid sitting out there, wide-eyed and gapemouthed, figuring I reckon he was bearing witness to a suicide by solo.

Harley finished, I give another little prayer and sit down, Harley come forward again. Said, "Will the congregation rise?" Waited till they done it, said, "Folks, this here revival ain't supported by no church or missionary group. Me and Brother Claude Dee depends on good christian folks like you to keep us on the road to glory. Right now Sister Henry is going to pass among you and take up a love offering. Search your hearts and give freely of your earthly goods. Like it says in the book of Leviticus, If thy brother be waxen poor, thou shalt relieve him, yea though he be a stranger and a sojourner, that he may live with thee." I give him that last part, changing it around a little.

Harley set in on "Living For Jesus" and Henry got up and went over to the runny-eyed old cooter, holding out the tin plate. Bout then's when he closed his eyes and raised his face towards heaven, moving his lips around like he was deep in prayer.

Henry waited him out. Harley finished the first verse and started in on the second. The old man went ahead praying, Henry was still waiting. Then I seen her reach out and give him a pretty good poke in the belly, knocking him a little off balance. Thought, Lordamighty, Henry, we ain't going to fill no coffers thataway. Which we wasn't, because the old cooter stood there a minute looking hell fire and damnation at Henry, then he slammed his hat on his head and walked out the back end of the tent. Henry yelled something at him but I couldn't make out what it was due to Harley's rackety singing.

Henry went ahead passing among them but Mrs. Dickerson was the onliest one that made a contribution. Henry come back up there, holding out the offering for me to bless it. I stood up, seen that lone dime in there, said, "I don't reckon we'll trouble the Lord with that tonight."

Congregation got sit back down, I come forward and read them scriptures I'd wrote on a piece of paper. Went, My beloved is mine and I am his, he pastures his flock among the lilies, turn, my beloved, until the day breathes and the shadows flee, be like a gazelle or a young stag upon rugged mountains, behold you are beautiful, my love, your lips are like a scarlet thread and your mouth is lovely, you are stately as a palm tree and your breasts are like its clusters, oh, I will climb the palm tree and lay hold of its branches, your breasts are like clusters of the vine and your kisses like fine wine that glides over lips and teeth, let us go out early to the vineyards whither the grape blossoms have opened and the pomegranates are in bloom, there I will give you my love.

To my thinking there ain't nothing in the bible sweeter than the book of Solomon. Hearing them words read out loud went straight to my heart. Had to take a minute to pull myself together again.

Harley come up behind me, whispered, "This here's where I sing another solo."

I said, "Sit down, Harley, you done dealt the Lord enough misery with your singing for one night."

Preached my main sermon. Started off by just stating my primary belief, which is that we're all sinners, ain't one of us that's not a sinner, born to it, sinners all our lives long, all going to die sinners. Said that being the case, I didn't see nothing wrong with having a little pleasure along the way. The gospel according to what you *can* do. Said if that meant drinking a can of beer now and then, a little casual fornication within reason, things like that, I didn't think nobody was going to die and go to hell for it. Talked on there a little about fornicative revelation, said the key to my primary belief was the words "within reason." Said you couldn't just go around fornicating all over the place, that you needed to use some common sense. Said that's where the revelation come in, that if you'd put your mind to it and open up your heart, it would generally be revealed to you which fornication was a sin and which wasn't.

Talked a little longer on that, rounded her off by coming back to the book of Solomon, said, "Now in that scripture I read before, it don't come right out and say them lovers fornicated, but they ain't one of us present but what knows that's what they done. Right there at the end, where he says, let us go out in the vineyard amidst the grape blossoms and pomegranates and I will give you my love, there aint no doubt but what they're about two pants away from fornication."

The kid had fell asleep, his daddy had been looking at his watch off and on for the last fifteen minutes, seen I hadn't set nobody afire with my first sermon. Told them I'd appreciate it they'd pass along the word that we was holding a revival and hoped they'd come back the next night. Then dismissed them.

Harley come up in a dither, said, "Damn it, we ain't sung the invitation hymn yet."

I said, "We ain't going to save no souls tonight, Harley, I got a feel for them things."

Man, his wife and kid, went straggling off, Mrs. Dickerson was still waiting back there, watching me with them panther eyes.

Told Harley to take the car, run into town try to find us some baloney and crackers, maybe pick up a six pack for me and him, couple of sody pops for Henry. Said, "You can work up a mortal appetite spreading the gospel."

Harley said, "I reckon that's why you see so many fat preachers."

Went back there to where Mrs. Dickerson was waiting, asked was there something I could do for her.

She said, "I was wondering could you walk me down the hill to the house, sometimes Mr. Dickerson lets that mean bull run loose in the meadow."

Thought, Lordamercy, this here might be the night we close down the mine shaft. Said, "Well, I wouldn't want no mean bull to get you."

We was leaving, I looked back, seen Henry standing there giving me the V for victory sign.

We walked a little ways, not saying nothing. A sweet night for surrender, crickets singing off in the darkness, air heavy with the smell of cut clover, a silver moon hanging above the willows along the creek.

A little ways on Mrs. Dickerson said, "That was a mighty fine sermon you preached."

I said, "Well, I thank you."

She said, "You read them scriptures, I might near busted out crying. Part about her breasts hanging down like clusters, how she give him her love and all."

Thought, don't jump too quick, boy, this here's a delicate situation. Said, "Yes, mam, them's beautiful scriptures all right."

Walked a little on, she said, "You really think them lovers fornicated, like you said?"

I said, "Stands to reason, don't it? Up there in that meadow amid them sweet smelling pomegranates, both of them unclad, the scriptures is pretty clear on that. Says, your navel is like a rounded bowl, your belly is a heap of wheat encircled with lilies. Says, make haste, my beloved, and be like a gazelle or a young stag upon the mountains of spices. That there's your language of love, and love without fornication ain't nothing but a hand-shake."

She stopped and stood there a good little while looking at me, then her voice not much more than a whisper she said, "Brother Claude Dee, you've give me something to dream about, something so deep down it hurts my heart." Didn't say nothing for a minute, then said, "I'll be at the service tomorrow night, and I thank you for walking me home."

I said, "Well, I'll just walk you on to the door, that bull ain't in the meadow, no telling where he's at."

A pretty dumb thing to say but I seen my conquest of this here femme fatal was maybe slipping away.

She said, "Not tonight, Mr. Dickerson's light's still on, I reckon he's waiting up for me."

Looked like I couldn't roll nothing but snake-eyes, said, "Mrs. Dickerson, I want to help you with your troubled soul, that's what I'm here for, why don't we just sink down here on this soft sward and open up our hearts to the benign indifference of the universe." Got that last from one of them books I read up at Pordell.

Mrs. Dickerson said, "I'd be too scared, out here in the moonlight. Mr. Dickerson's one of them anxious husbands. We don't sleep together or nothing but he caught me out with some other man, ain't no telling what he'd do."

Before I could say anything to that, she give me a peck on the cheek, went running off towards the stile at the end of the meadow.

Stood there a little watching. Thought, Mrs. Dickerson, this here conquest is over, cause it don't take no very smart man to figure out the fucking I'm getting ain't worth the fucking I'm taking.

Went back up the hill, found Henry in the tent picking her toes. She'd lit one of the lanterns we'd brought along, looked sitting there in the soft yellow glow like a sweet picture of innocence.

Give me a slant look, said, "That didn't take long."

I said, "Well, Henry, it ain't but about three hundred yards down to that stile."

She said, "Way she was looking at you during the preaching, I figured she was ready for a good screwing."

I said, "Henry, that ain't the way we talk around here. I'm a minister of the gospel, I'll ask you to keep that in mind."

She said, "What's that got to do with screwing Mrs. Dickerson?"

I said, "Henry."

She said, "Mr. Davenport used to screw mama on the back porch, broad daylight. I'd watch them through the kitchen window . . . ."

I said, "Henry."

Wasn't no stopping her, said, "Mr. Davenport weighed about three hundred pounds, mama not no bigger than a half growed garter snake, looked like a grizzly bear fucking a sweet tator vine . . . ."

I said, "Henry, I ain't going to listen to no more of that trashy talk."

She said, "Once he was out there humping mama, Mrs. Cordell's old black dog come up, seen what they was doing . . . ."

I didn't hear no more, cause I walked out of that tent her still talking. Went up to a grassy knoll above the persimmon grove, sit down and done some serious thinking. One thing I thought, with everything else I had on my mind about the biggest problem I faced at the moment was rehabilitating Henry.

Sit awhile watching all them stars twinkling in the sky, a kind of sadness come over me, though I couldn't think of nothing special to be sad about. It's like some secret self inside you is yearning for something you ain't got and don't even know what it is and maybe won't never know. I got to wondering what things give me the most pleasure, and where I come out was maybe my pleasures was mostly behind me. Trouble with that, if pleasures is all behind you, they ain't nothing but memories. Man ain't got nothing but memories to hold onto might as well call in the hounds and give up the hunt. Give myself a little talking to, said, shit, boy, don't nothing never come to them that sits and broods, whatever it is you're yearning for you're going to have to find your ownself, pissing and moaning ain't going to bring you nothing but more grief.

Didn't help much. Times you just got to wait them deep feelings out.

Heard the car coming up through the meadow, a little later seen Harley get out and go in the tent carrying a paper poke. Wasn't yet ready for one of them gibberty conversations with Harley so stayed where I was at.

Awhile later he come out of the tent, come up there to where I was sitting, said, "I thought you was hungry."

I said, "There's a couple of things I got to think through, I'll eat in a little."

He didn't say nothing for a minute, then said, "I reckon you want to be alone."

I said, "You reckon right."

Still didn't leave, then started snickering to hisself, said, "Henry tell you bout the time some fellar was fucking her mama, dog come and bit him on the ass?"

I said, "Harley, I done killed one man, you ain't far from being number two."

Woken next morning to black skies, thunder rumbling above the hills off to the west, said, to Harley, "This here's one of them dismal dark days that makes you think of far off places and lonely women.

Harley said, "Makes me think of hayloft fucking."

Times with Harley I wished I'd just kept my thoughts to myself. Sent him into town to put more signs in the store windows announcing my sermon for that night, which was, SIN AIN'T NOTHING BUT SATAN ROLLING SEVEN. Didn't have no idea how I was going to work that into the gospel according to what you *can* do, but figured I needed something that would get their attention. Thought anyhow I could come up with something before time to preach. Told Harley to walk the streets after he'd put up the signs, talk to people, see could he work up some interest in our meeting.

After he'd left, went back in the tent, seen Henry sitting there on a camp stool drinking a can of Lone Star we'd had left over. Said, "Ain't you a little young to be swilling beer?"

She didn't give me no answer to that, after a little said, "Where you come from?"

I said, "Down the road aways."

She give me a long steady look, said, "You ain't no real preacher are you?"

I said, "What the hell does that mean?"

She said, "It's a feeling I got. I seen lots of preachers in my time, Baptists, Holy Rollers, all kinds. You ain't like none of them."

I said, "Well, I reckon your feelings done led you astray this time, cause it happens I been duly ordained by the church of the Holy Witness."

She said, "Yeah, where's that at?"

I said, "Don't make no difference where it's at, I ain't bounden to explain nothing to you."

She sit a little looking at me, said, "You ain't never preached before last night have you?"

I said, "Look, Henry, I done told you not to push too hard on me. You ain't nothing but a scrawny-assed kid that come wandering up that hill yesterday because your mama sent you. I taken you in with a glad heart because the gospel commands me to succor the weak and downtrodden, says, Though I speak with the tongues of men and angels, and have no charity, I am become as sound brass or tinkling cymbals."

She said, "Cram it."

I said, "Henry, that there's a phrase of yours that don't set well with me."

She took a swig of beer, said, "You want to know why you ain't going to save nobody?"

I said, "No, but I reckon I'm going to find out."

She said, "People wants to be damned. That's what they come for, them that's saved and them that ain't. You're standing up there telling people it don't matter what they do, telling them that they can screw anything that walks, talks, or crawls, and there ain't nobody can say it's wrong. Even trying to make out the bible ain't against fornication. Truth is, the bible says fornicators is going to die and go straight to hell, I heard it preached on many a time. That's what you ought to be a telling them people, scare the living piss out of them. Reason people join the church ain't cause they want to go to heaven, that stuff about them streets being paved wih gold, how they ain't no suffering or sickness up there, ain't nobody believes that crap.

Fear's what it is, people join the church cause they're scared of going to hell."

I said, "Well, I reckon you better just leave the preaching to me, Henry, I been called to it."

She said, "J.D. says the plow handles has lost many a good man to the Lord's call."

Didn't care to hear no more of that so went out back and studied the storm clouds. Getting darker by the minute, wind rising, now and then a flash of streaky lightning cutting across the sky. Weather that sets you to thinking, put in my mind that maybe there was more to preaching than I first had thought. Thought anyways Henry was right about one thing, I wasn't no regular preacher. What I was was Claude Dee Moran Junior, a piss poor and maybe misguided sonofabitch who shot and killed his best friend and paid his mortal penance, who sit in that goddam cell up at Pordell four years, seven months. and some odd days, waiting for them to one day open the door and say, all right, boy, you can go now.

Decided right then I wasn't no more going to preach the gospel according to what you *can* do, or the gospel according to what you *can't* do, or no other kind of gospel I didn't know nothing about. Decided to just tell people who I was and where I been and what I seen along the way. The gospel according to doing the best you can.

Little later seen the rain a coming, a solid grey sheet sweeping up across the meadow, blowed by the wind. Stood there waiting till it come, let it wash over me like the waters of the river Jordan. Not by works of righteousness are we saved, but by the washing of regeneration and renewing of the holy ghost.

━━━━━━━━━━

Rained steady most of the day, then around four the clouds begin to break up and patches of blue sky showed through. Me and Henry went and sit on a log up the rise and eat the baloney and cheese that was left over and listened to the birds singing sweet songs in the persimmon grove.

Didn't say nothing for awhile, then Henry said, "You ain't wondering what happened to Harley?"

I said, "I try not to never wonder what's happened to Harley."

She said, "He ain't very bright, is he?"

I said, "Well, he ain't no doctor Epstein, that's what you mean."

Sit a little, said, "What's your mama going to think, you don't come home?"

She said, "Ain't going to think nothing. Ain't the first time I've went off. Joined up once with a carnival that come through town, stayed gone two months. Man named Buford run a dice cage, said he was going to make a shill out of me, pay me twenty dollars a week. Worked out all right till he got drunk one night and tried to get in my pants. I said, fuck your ownself and come on home."

I said, "Henry, I wonder could we just have a brief discussion about the way you talk?"

She said, "What's wrong with the way I talk?"

I said, "Mainly some of them words you use is just a trifle unladylike."

She said, "I ain't no lady."

I said, "Ain't yet. Will be. It's time you give it some serious thought."

She sit a good little while turning that over, said, "Do you like a woman better she's a lady?"

I said, "Yes, mam, truth is I do."

She give me a long look, said "Well, then I'll think about it."

Thought, Lordamighty, what's come over Henry. Said, "Well, I thank you."

Come six o'clock Harley still hadn't come back. Henry went down to direct traffic, I went up in the persimmon grove to do a little serious meditating. About half a hour later Harley come driving up, seen him get out and look in the tent, then he come up the rise to the persimmon grove, walking I thought a little wavery. Come over to where I was, just stood there a silly grin on his face, not saying nothing. Seen I was right, he was pecker deep in the sauce.

I said, "You're a mess, ain't you?"

He said, "You talking to me?"

Said, "You get them signs put up?"

He said, "Yep."

Said, "Tell them people they ought to come to our revival?"

He said, "Yep. Told them it beat sitting around the house with a hard on."

I said, "Where'd you get the money to buy whatever it is you been swilling?"

He said, "Sold the spare tire and rear view mirror off the car. Got a dollar and some change left, you want it."

He'd just about pushed too hard on me, said, "What I want's you to go and get back in that goddam car, don't come out till after the service is over."

He said, "What about my solos?"

I said, "They ain't going to be no solos. You need sleep a hellova lot worse than the world needs your croaking."

Seen I'd cut him to the quick. He stood there a little looking like a spanked spaniel, said, "Trouble with you, Claude Dee, you ain't got no forgiveness in your heart." Give me a doleful look, shook his head, said, "And you call yourself a preacher." Slunk off back down the rise.

Might a been I was too hard on him, but like the bible says, Thou shalt not befoul the house of the Lord. Something like that.

I went back down to the tent a little later, looked like maybe I owed Harley an apology. Counted three pickups, four cars, and a log truck parked down at the lower end of the meadow. Inside the tent there was maybe eighteen or twenty people sitting around on the grass, one of which was Mrs. Dickerson, sitting down close to the front, her leg hitched a little up, flashing that pound of pearly flesh.

Told myself to just keep my mind on what I was doing, said to the congregation that tonight we was going to dispense with the prayer and singing, that I just wanted to read a short scripture and then say some things that lay heavy on my heart. Read from the book of Deuteronomy, goes, Be strong and of good courage, fear not, for the Lord thy God, he it is that doth go with thee, he will not fail thee nor forsake thee.

Then give my sermon. Told them I'd been in prison, didn't say for what, that it was there closed in by them cold grey walls that I seen the light, that there admist the weeping and gnashing of teeth I heard the voice, that there, blind and cast in darkness, I opened my heart to the sweet song of the dove, that there among the downtrodden and outcast I wrestled the angel of Jacob and cried out for deliverance from my mortal sins.

Went on like that a little, then told them the story of Buford McHenry, a man up at Pordell condemned to die for killing his own baby girl, how the chaplain went every morning and prayed with him but Buford had hardened his heart and wouldn't repent what he done, how the day before he was to fry he taken Jesus as his personal savior, how when they led him away the next day he walked to his mortal death shouting hallelujah and praise the Lord.

Said, "Buford McHenry died brave, same as Steven in the bible, rocked to death one cold rainy day in December, same as Uriah, sent to die in battle by one of them wicked kings that coveted his woman, same as Daniel, throwed in a dungeon and clawed to death by lions." Said, "Right there's a truth needs thinking on, living ain't nothing but learning how to die, the gospel according to dying brave . . . ."

About then somewheres outside Harley come to life, all of a sudden cut loose on "Onward Christian Soldiers," sounded like the wail of a coyote off in the night, and coming closer.

Seen the congregation looking at each other then at me, figuring I reckon they'd been beset by a banshee.

Thought, Harley, I hope you had a good day cause you ain't going to see another one. Said to the congregation, "Ladies and gentlemen, that sweet sound you hear is the voice of my songmaster, Brother Harley Biggs, struck down this morning by a severe case of intestinal pneumonia, told by a doctor to take to his bed lest he endanger his very life, onliest thing that doctor don't know is Brother Harley's faith is stronger than your modern medicine, a faith more precious than gold that perisheth, verily a faith that moveth mountains . . . ."

Seen Henry sitting off to one side, her face squinched up like she was about to bust out laughing. Give her a stern look.

About then Harley come through the tent opening, walking stiff legged like a zombie, singing at the top of his lungs. Walked past me, stopped in front of the congregation, opened out his arms like Abraham calling to his bosom the lost children of Egypt. Set in on another verse, Like a mighty army, moves the church of God, Brothers we are treading, where the saints have trod.

I motioned Henry to pass the collection pan, stepped up beside Harley, started clapping in time with the music.

Henry passed among them. Seen people reaching for their pockets. Thought, Lordamercy, we done touched some wayward hearts.

Henry finished taking up the collection, come down for me to say a blessing over it. Harley kept on a singing, run out of verses, started over again. I seen his eyes was a little glazed over, wondered had he fell into some kind of trance. Waited him out a little but seen he'd done got the bit between his teeth, put my hand gentle on the back of his neck, waited till he come to the end of the verse, shouted out, "Brother Harley's going to sing one more verse, this here's the *last verse!*" At the same time clamped down on Harley's neck, trying to break the spell that had come over him. Must a clamped down harder than I meant to, he yanked loose, stood there staring at me like I was somebody he hadn't never seen before, then turned and walked out of the tent.

I said a little prayer over the offering, thanked everybody for coming, then announced my sermon for the next night. Which was, HOW TO GIRD YOUR LOINS AND KEEP THEM GIRDED.

Dismissed the congregation and went outside looking for Harley, but he wasn't nowhere around so I sit down and done a little thinking. Some reason I felt a kind of emptiness inside. Thought of Ada, which didn't help none.

Little later Henry come out there, stood a minute looking at me, said, "Mrs. Dickerson was waiting for you, she just left."

I said, "Fine."

She said, "You don't fuck her, somebody else will."

Hopeless, Henry was.

She said, "We took in four dollars and twenty-six cents tonight." I didn't say nothing to that, she said, "We're having a interesting talk, ain't we?"

I said, "Henry, I'm done talked out."

After a little she said, "We ain't had a square meal since I joined up with you. Maybe we oughta drive into town and spend that collection on some meat and taters."

Standing there, little snit of a girl, not no bigger than a peavine. Figured maybe it was time I thought about somebody beside my ownself, said, "I ain't got no better idea. Let's see can we find Harley."

Which we couldn't. Looked about half an hour, out in the persimmon grove, up the rise above the tent, even walked down to the creek at the lower end of the meadow.

Henry said, "How come you're so worried about Harley, looks to me like he don't do nothing but screw things up."

I said, "Harley's Harley." Truth was Harley grew on you. Mostly like fungus, but me and him went back aways.

Finally we give up the search, got in the car and drove down the rise. Got to the gate, seen Harley standing at the fence off to one side staring at the darkness. I got out and went over there he didn't look around.

I said, "We been looking for you."

He said, "I reckon you want me to go on back home."

I said, "Ain't nobody said nothing about going home. Get in the car, we're going to get something to eat."

He said, "You ain't still mad?"

I said, "Get in the car, Harley."

He said, "You want me to go on home, I will."

I said, "Get in the car, Harley."

He got in the back seat and we set out for town, drove along there awhile, nobody saying nothing, then Harley said, "Henry, tell Claude Dee about that fellar fucking your mama, got bit in the ass by a dog."

———————————

Next night turned out to be a bell ringer. First, looked like me and Harley had set Caledonia off in a wave of revival fever. Come preaching time they must a been forty or fifty people scattered around on the grass. Seen Mrs. Dickerson was back, decked out in a sheeny yellow dress, so tight looked like her ass was held in bondage.

I prayed and Harley sung a couple of solos, then I give my sermon. Read first a scripture from Deuteronomy, went, Be strong and of good courage, fear not nor be afraid of them, for the Lord thy God will not fail thee nor forsake thee.

Started off by saying they was lots of folks didn't have no idea what a girded loin meant, said girded loins was a deep subject, they was even some preachers that didn't understand it. Said you could anoint your loins with precious oils from the distant lands of Arabia, bind them up with bamboo strips from the river Nile, they still wouldn't necessarily be girded.

Went on awhile with that, then got off on the story of David and the giant, how one of them kings, Sampson I think it was, and the Israelites was at war with the Philistines, how things had come to a standstill because the Philistines had went over to Cana and hired a giant name of Goliath to be their hit man. There they was, the Israelites lined up on one side of the creek, the Philistines on the other, little rain drizzling down. Then out come this giant, little over nine feet tall, give a mighty dare, asked was they any of them Israelites wanted to take him on in open combat. Course the Israelites was all looking at each other, saying, you go, I don't want to take on no giant, things like that. About then was when this scrawny little kid name of David come walking out. Had a bean flip in his hand, couldn't a been more than fourteen, fifteen years old. Giant seen him coming up there, seen that bean flip in his hand, he busted out laughing, said, little pissant like you come to slay me have you? All them Philistines started laughing, even some of the Israelites was snickering, but old David just bent down slow and easy, picked him out a rock about the size of a golf ball, put it in his bean flip, taken aim and let her fly. Caught that scutter right between the eyes, he hit the ground like a stuck hog, slewed forevermore. Them Philistines seen what happened, they took off running like a herd of spooked prairie dogs, yelling, David done slayed Goliath! David done slayed Goliath! King Sampson and the Israelites run up there where David was standing, gathered around him yelling, you done saved us from certain death and damnation, old David just smiled, shrugged it off, said, somebody had to do it.

Summed her up, said, "Now right there's your classic example, David went up there with his loins girded, and what that means is he wasn't scared of that giant or nothing else, so the way it comes out is, having girded loins is just another way of saying you ain't afraid of nothing or nobody. The gospel according to doing what you have to do. Let us pray."

Harley sung another solo, Henry passed among them with the collection pan. I went and sit on the camp stool and closed my eyes, wore out from all that raving and ranting.

Harley finished singing I come forward, he leaned over said, "You want me to sing my invitation hymn now?"

I said, "Not tonight, Harley, I'll just wrap her up with a little prayer."

Truth was I'd been giving that some hard thinking, and where I come out was I didn't feel exactly right about inviting people to give their lives to the Lord. Figured if in my preaching I said something that caused them to change their ways of living that was fine, but making out the only way they could be saved was to come up there and get my blessings was another matter.

After the service was over I went up the hill aways, sit and listened to the sweet sounds of darkness coming on. A hush over the meadow, crickets singing along the creek bank, little breeze stirring, soft as the touch of a sad hearted woman.

One of them moments, hallowed and holy.

Seen Henry coming up the hill, holding in her hand a folded piece of paper.

Got up there she said, "We took in nine dollars, sixty-two cents, and this note." Held it out, said, "Mrs. Dickerson put it in the collection pan."

I took the note, sit a minute watching her, seen she was waiting me out, said, "Henry, is this here note wrote to you?"

She said, "How would I know who it's wrote to?"

I said, "Well, why don't you just go on back to the tent, see if they's something you can maybe help Harley with, this note's wrote to you, I'll let you know."

She said, "It's wrote to you. I done read it." Went back down the hill moving slow.

Read Mrs. Dickerson's sad message in the twilight, said:

Dear Brother Claude Dee,

I am in distress. Mr. Dickerson has gone over to Delmar to buy some hogs. He won't be back till tomorrow. The door on the wellporch ain't locked. I wonder could you come tonight and give me comfort.

Latressa Dickerson

Waited up there till it was good dark, went back down to the tent, seen Harley and Henry playing pinocle by lantern light.

They sit eyeing me like two beagle hounds that's got a snake cornered. I said, "Mrs. Dickerson's somehow worked herself into a state, says she needs some pastoral counseling. It ain't something I want to do but I reckon it's a part of my job."

Henry sit there grinning like a chessie cat, Harley said,

"You got plenty of condoms?"

Didn't have time to start in on Harley so went ahead on down the rise, keeping a close lookout for Dickerson's meanbull. A little ways from the house seen a light at a upstairs window, no sign of Dickerson's pickup truck. Crossed the stile and went in slow, counting shadows. Thought, ain't no woman alive worth a ass full of buckshot. Come to the wellporch, stood a little listening, couldn't hear nothing but the breeze rustling honeysuckle along the fencerow, far off the lorn baying of a dog. Went on up, tried the door, unlocked like Mrs. Dickerson said. Eased her open, seen a dimlit room, at the far end a stairway. Moved along there like a chicken thief in a henhouse, got to the top of the stairs, stood a minute listening to my pounding heart. Seen under a door at the end of the hall a sliver of light, went down there, give a little tap, Mrs. Dickerson invited me to come on in. Opened the door, seen her laying there on the bed, them panther eyes shining, a sheet pulled up over her tender body.

Took a breath, said, "Well, mam, I got your message."

She dropped her eyes, said, "I reckon you think I'm something naughty."

I said, "No, mam, I don't. Judge not lest ye be judged."

Could a counted ten, that room quiet as a monk's cell, all of a sudden she flang that sheet away, wasn't wearing nothing but a gold wedding ring, said, "Save me, Brother Claude Dee, for I am a sinner."

I said, "Yes, mam, we're all sinners in the eyes of the Lord."

Turned out the light, surrendered myself to the soft and nubile bosom of Mrs. Latressa Dickerson.

━━━━━━━

Next morning Harley was down at the creek taking a bath, me and Henry was cleaning the sparkplugs in the

Dodge, seen Mr. Dickerson coming over the stile at the
lower end of the meadow. Figured he was coming to collect
the rent due him. Figured wrong. He got a little closer I
seen the look on his face, mouth closed tight as the blade
of a shut knife, thought, that sure as hell ain't the look
of a man coming after overdue rent.

He come on up there, walking fast, stopped and give
me a fierce look, taken a folded piece of yellow paper out
of his hip pocket, held it out, said, "This here yours, Mr.
Preacher?"

Seen even before I took it in hand it was some notes I'd
jotted down for my girding the loins sermon, looked it
over careful, thinking fast, said, "Yessir, this here's some
sermon notes of mine. How might you a come by them?"

He said, "Come by them down there on my wellporch,
come by them and know how they got there."

Thought of an old Pordell saying about sloven lovers,
goes, fuck at midnight, hang at dawn.

Said, "No, sir, I think I can explain how them notes got
down there. Yesterday afternoon I went to return the lard
can Mrs. Dickerson had kindly let me . . . ."

Cut me off, said, "Listen, you lowlife sonofabitch, I done
talked to Mrs. Dickerson, come down hard on her, she's
done confessed what happened . . . ."

Cut him off, borrowing time, said, "Well, sir, just let me
say this . . . ."

Cut me off again, said, "You ain't got nothing to say I
want to hear." Then talking slow and deliberate he said,
"You got till sundown to pack up that goddam tent and
move off my land. I got a twelve guage pumpgun down
there and enough buckshot to blow your ass to kingdom
come. That's where you want to go, just hang around till
the sun goes down."

He turned and walked off down the rise, walking so fast

he was kind of stumbling along.

I looked at Henry, she was looking at me. Wasn't nothing said for a couple of minutes. Point was, Dickerson wasn't nobody to tamper with. One thing I learned up at Pordell is how to tell if a man will kill you or if he won't. It's mostly in the eyes.

I said, "Well, looks like our first revival's done come to a sudden halt."

Henry give me a look, like she couldn't believe what she'd heard, said, "What! You telling me you're going to let that dried old fart run you off?"

I said, "Well now, Henry, I don't see as I've got no big lot of choices." She sit there shaking her head, I said, "Exactly what would you suggest?"

She said, "We'll shoot it out with him. My uncle Jess lives about three miles on down this road. He's got a shotgun and a 30-30 rifle. He works at the sawmill up town but I know where they're kept. We get them guns, hide up there in that persimmon grove, old man Dickerson comes up that rise, be *his* ass gets blowed to kingdom come."

I said, "Henry, I knowed lots of little girls in my time, I'd have to say you ain't one of the smarter ones."

About then Harley come walking up, said, "What's all this talk about guns?"

Henry said, "Old man Dickerson found out Claude Dee give his wife a fucking, come up here, told him to fold up his tent and get out of town, give him till . . . ."

I said, "Henry, just kindly let me do the talking."

Harley said, "You didn't take nothing off him did you?"

Henry said, "Ha! You should a seen him, standing there stammering like a kid caught jacking off in the corn bin."

I said, "Henry, I told you about pushing on me."

Nothing was said for a little, then Harley said, "So we're packing her in, that what you're saying?"

I said, "That's what I'm saying, so just get over there

and start pulling up them tent stakes."

Harley stood a minute like he was thinking it over, said, "Well, I reckon you're the boss."

I said, "I reckon you're right."

Harley went shuffling off, Henry was still sitting there watching me.

I said, "That means you too. There ain't no free boarders around here. You don't want to pull your weight, then pack up your scrawny ass and get on home."

About a minute passed, me and her locked in a eye fight, then a little grin come on her face. She said, "Well, I reckon they's one thing we both know, you won't be humping old hot pants Dickerson no more." Got up and went over to the tent, started yanking at a tiedown stake.

Like Harley said, she was some Henry.

Chapter Five

Next day drove into Howtown after Aunt Heather, we stopped at the commissary bought hog jowl, sweet taters, corn, cowpeas, some other stuff, went back to the farm, her and Henry cooked up a fitten supper.

Me and Harley was having a beer on the back porch, not saying nothing, then Harley said, "You worried about that dog, ain't you?"

Truth was I was. Come home the day before he wasn't there, went a mile or more along the creek yelling for him, he still hadn't showed up when morning come. He'd run off, that was one thing. A dire accident had befell him, that was something else.

Also, I was a little worried about our financial condition. We had maybe forty, fifty dollars left, no benches or songbooks, batmobile needing tires.

Then a bright thought come to me, said, "Harley, what worries me, you want to know, is we ain't got but a few dollars in our revival budget."

Harley said, "Yeah, well."

I let her hang there a minute, said, "How much you reckon that house of yours would bring on the open market."

Harley said, "Ain't my house, belongs to mama."

I said, "Harley, your mama's been dead two years, she ain't going to need no house where she's at."

He said, "Where you thinking she's at?"

Hard to keep Harley to the point, said, "I'm thinking she's in her heavenly dwelling place, where she shall not hunger or thirst, neither shall the heat or the sun smite her."

He shook his head, said, "I don't know. How come ever time we run out of money we sell something belongs to me?"

I said, "For the simple reason I ain't got nothing worth selling."

He said, "How come we don't sell this here cockleburr farm?"

It just come out, said, "Did, we wouldn't have no place to live."

He give me a look, said, "You saying I'm going to move out here with you?"

Thought, Lordamighty, ain't no sacrifice too great, said, "That's what I got in mind."

He sit a minute, said, "I don't know. What if someday I get married?"

Said, "Shit, Harley, we ain't going to get nowhere we sit round waiting on a miracle to happen."

About then Henry come out there, red-faced and sweaty from her labors in that hot kitchen, said, "Your dog come home yet?"

I said, "Not yet."

Must a sounded lorn, she said, "You ain't done nothing since we got here but pine for that dumb dog."

I said, "Damn it, I ain't pining. I got out of the pining business awhile back."

She said, "Your Aunt Heather says you wasn't fit for nothing, you was a boy."

I said, "Well, boys ain't supposed to be fit for nothing."

She said, "Says you was always in some kind of meanness."

I said, "Henry, ain't there something else you can help with in the kitchen?"

She said, "Says you was always fiddle fucking around when you should a been going to school."

I said, "Aunt Heather never said nothing about fiddle fucking around, that there's some of your trashy talk. I never said I was no Little Lord Falteroy but I wasn't no worse than most."

She said, "Your mama still alive?"

That's when something come over me, I don't know exactly what, but I didn't care to talk no more with Henry or Harley or nobody else. Got up and walked off, down through the field to the creek, turned there, kept on a walking till I come to the pole bridge down below where the fox fern grows. Sit down on a log and let my mind run free.

Thing was, all them years up at Pordell I tried not to think about Larry Lee and what I done. What you face in the pen is just getting up in the morning and brooding over what can't be changed. But sometimes I'd remember how it was before I come up on him and Ada that morning, how me and him would hunt squirrels down in Caney river bottom, sitting in a hickernut grove listening for cuttings, smoking, talking quiet about one thing and another. What it was was, we was best friends. I'd a caught somebody else fucking my Ada, chances are I wouldn't a done what I done. Which was, I seen them hammerlocked on that bed and went for a couple of minutes out of my mind.

Thought, it don't matter, whatever happens happens. Thought, comes times to meet my maker I'll just say, you know what I done and why I done it, I ain't asking for no special favors.

Little later heard somebody coming along the creek path, looked up seen Henry walking slow through the trees. She come over here, stood a good little while without saying nothing, said, "I made you mad, I'm sorry."

I said, "It don't matter."

She said, "Does to me."

I said, "I reckon we all have to face the truth, ain't no place you can hide."

She said, "Aunt Heather said whatever you done, didn't nothing change the way she felt. Said you was a good hearted boy, always ready to help them that couldn't help theirselves." Couldn't think of nothing to say to that, she said, "I reckon you don't like me anymore." Waited a little, said, "You want me to go on home, just say so."

Her and Harley. I said, "Ain't nobody said nothing about you going home."

She sit down on the other end of the log and we sit awhile not talking, listening to sounds along the creek. Bream popping insects long the bank, a slow humming in the trees, the drumbeats of a woodpecker working on a dead tree. The sweet sounds of life everlasting.

After awhile Henry said, "You still mad?"

I said, "I wasn't never mad."

Sit a little, she said, "You want to be by yourself?"

I said, "No. Long as you don't go off on one of them talking jags."

Sit a little longer, she said, "You don't want to hear about the time Brother Bledsoe caught mama and old man Davenport fucking on the kitchen floor?"

Next morning we drove into town, stopped at Barkley's hardware, bought paint, brushes, scrapers, borrowed from Tooter some carpenter tools, went down there and set in on Harley's house, Henry laying waste them bitter weeds, Harley doing the painting, me trying to shore up a buckled roof on the back porch.

Had worked maybe two hours, went around there to check on Harley, he seen me coming, all of a sudden sit down, stuck his head between his legs, started heaving like a cat spitting up hair balls.

Sounded like them heaves was a little worked at, stood there a minute, said, "Something ailing you, Harley?"

He said, "Heat stroke coming on." Sunk his head lower, said, "I can tell when one's coming, my breathing gets warped."

I said, "Well, I'll take it kindly you don't drop dead till after we've sold this here property."

He give me a slant look, said, "It ain't funny. I damn near died from heat strokes more than once. What you call your prone to it. What it is is all the fluids drains out of my system."

I said, "Ain't no problem, they's a bucket of water on the back porch."

He said, "Water don't do no good. Need something's got more kick to it."

Seen what he was getting at, so we took a break. Went up to the Eagle cafe, old Brenda come sidling over, I ordered a round of beers.

She said, "Claude Dee, you know I can't serve that kid no beer."

I said, "Miss Henry ain't no kid. Twenty-one years old, struck down she was twelve years old by a cruel affliction knowed as lymphoma gastritus, ain't growed a inch since."

She said, "Well, I hope it ain't catching." Said to Henry, You want a coke or something, hon?"

Cut in before Henry could devastate her with one of them famous smart ass remarks, said, "Just kindly put a six pack of them Lone Stars in a poke and we'll cash and carry."

She went to get the beer, Henry said, "Last time I seen tits like them was on Uncle Evert's holstein cow."

I said, "Henry, one of these days I'm going to get me some lye soap, give your mouth a good washing out."

She said, "You ain't never heard nobody say tits before?"

Lordy.

Went back down to the house, quaffed them beers, Harley's warped breathing come around. Set in again cleaning and fixing, come sundown you wouldn't knowed that place, looked like one of them Jim Walters giveaway homes.

Sent Harley to get another six pack, me and Henry sit on the back porch watching shadows come on soft in the fading sunlight. Off in a tree somewheres a mockingbird trilling, made you think of far off times when the world was easy.

After a little Henry said, "You decided yet where we aim to hold our next revival?"

I said, "I reckon soon as we sell this house that's something we'll have to figure out."

She said, "J.D. says the meanest town in south Arkansas is Dalton. He worked over there last summer at the sawmill, says them millhands gets drunk on Saturday night, raises all kinds of hell, says he never seen nothing like it, people getting shot, cut up . . . ."

I said, "Well now just a minute, Henry, what I am is a revival type preacher, sounds like what them people in Dalton needs is a lawman."

She said, "You're scared of a few drunken millhands, I'd say you ain't much of a preacher."

I said, "Damn it, Henry, I never said I was scared, just said I ain't a lawman."

Got to thinking about that though, what was a preacher's business and what wasn't, got to thinking about them money-changers in the bible, how they was befouling the temple, somebody went and told Jesus, he went over there and threw them fuckers out of that holy place. Give you something to think about.

Little later Harley come back, I said, "Harley, you ever been to Dalton?"

He said, "Ain't been, ain't got no plans to go. Fellar I know lived over there a couple of years, said a man that values his ass ain't got no business in Dalton." Give me a sideways look, said, "Why?"

I said, "Ain't no why, Harley, I was just asking."

Drunk another beer, wrote out a sign on one of them left over posters to put in the yard. French bungalow was Harley's idea. Sign said:

FOR SALE
FRENCH BUNGALOW—CHEAP
Contact Mr. Harley Biggs

We all went across the road and stood there a little looking at what our labors had wrought.

Harley said, "We done good, didn't we?"

I said, "Damn good, Harley. We done damn good."

Next day around noon me and Henry was sitting on the back steps out at the farm, Harley'd went into town to procure some groceries, sun beating down, heat coming up off them fields in shimmery waves.

I'd bout fell asleep, thought I seen some movement in the sumac down by the barn lot, had a sinking feeling deep inside, somehow knowed what it was. Minute later Elijah come through the bushes, dragging hisself along on his belly, one limp leg trailing behind, as pitiful a sight as ever I seen. We run down there he rolled over on his back, whimpering like a new whelped pup, seen in them sorrowful eyes he was suffering a mighty pain. One leg hanging by just a shred of skin, a deep gash in his neck, hair along his flank matted with blood, looked like he'd come out second best in a ax fight. Near bout tore my heart out.

Took my knife cut that shred of skin, left that leg a laying there, picked him up gentle and carried him to the house, laid him out the porch, told Henry to watch over him. Went and tore into strips one of Aunt Heather's sheets, got what booze was left in the bottle and a pan of water. Got back out there Henry was sitting with Elijah's bloody head in her lap, patting him and whispering comfort in his ear.

She give me a lornful look, said, "He ain't going to die is he?"

A Henry I hadn't never seen before. I said, "Does, it'll serve him right, running off like that, ain't got the sense of a barnyard guinea."

Cleaned them wounds best I could, poured some of Gussie's rotgut in the open cuts and bound them up. Seen blood was still oozing from the leg stump so made a tourniquet and tied it above the joint then wrapped the stub.

Carried him inside and laid him out on the bed, not whimpering no more, his eyes a little glazed over.

I looked at Henry, seen the hurt in her eyes, said, "They ain't nothing else we can do for him."

She went and sit on the side of the bed, just sit there looking at that poor maimed creature, after a little said, "He's going to die ain't he?"

I said, "He is or he ain't." She didn't say nothing more, I said, "Ain't no point in sitting there grieving over him." She still didn't say nothing so I went on out back.

Got to thinking about a poem I read up at Pordell. Man found a hawk with a busted wing, took it home, tried to nurse it back to life. Wasn't no use though, wasn't no way he could mend that busted wing, so he shot it. Give it the lead gift in the twilight, was the way it went. Bout broke his heart. Said, come right down to it, he'd sooner kill a man than a hawk.

A hawk or a dog, comes to the same thing. Gives you something to think about.

Couldn't a been five minutes later Henry come out there, stood a little looking off towards the mountains, said, "He's dead."

Went in there seen she was right, Elijah had done gone to his mortal rest. Carried him out back, told Henry to get a shovel out of the barn, we taken him down to the creek and buried him in the sweet shade of a pin oak tree.

Got him covered up, we stood there quite a little while. Wasn't nothing to say. Henry was staring at the grave, her face hardset as a dried buckeye, finally she said, "You ain't going to say no words over him?"

I said, "No." Wasn't much of a answer but it would a took too long to explain.

She give me a long hard look, said, "You don't grieve for nothing or nobody do you?"

Didn't have no answer for that one either.

━━━━━━━━━━

Next morning we was planting wild flowers in the front yard, Henry's idea, looked up seen a car coming along the drive leading up the house. Car stopped and a woman got out. Wearing overhauls, one of them rawbone titless women, hadn't looked twice you'd a thought she was a man.

Come striding over there, said pretty businesslike, "Which one of you gentlemen is Mr. Biggs?"

Harley said, "That there would be me."

She said, "Name's Onell Cartwright, real estate dealer over at Delmar. Man up town tells me you got a property for sale."

Harley said, "Told you right, French bungalow, pecan tree in the backyard, inside plumbing, sitting on half a acre . . . ."

Cut him off, said, "Why don't we just have a look at it, I ain't got time for no sale pitch."

She followed us into town, we got down to Harley's she got out, had a flashlight in her hand, went and crawled up under the house, communing with them spiders and snakes for about twenty minutes. Come out bespoiled, hair full of cobwebs, went inside, stomped around on the floor, shaken the windows to see was they tight in the frames, finally come over to Harley, said, "What you asking?"

Harley give his rotten teeth a suck, said, "Twenty thousand."

Henry give me a look, turned square around and walked out. Thought, Lordamighty, Harley's mind's done gone out of business.

Mrs. Cartwright was looking at Harley like he'd just let go a global fart. Said, "Did you say twenty thousand?"

Harley said, "That's what I said. Fresh painted, hot and cold running water . . . ."

I said, "Harley, if I might just get in a word here, maybe we ought to let Mrs. Cartwright make us a offer . . . ."

Harley said, "This here's mama's house, I ain't even sure now I want to sell . . . ."

Mrs. Cartwright said, "Three thousand."

Harley said, "Goddam it . . . ."

I said, "Harley." Said to Mrs. Cartwright, "Are we talking cash money?"

She said, "Cash money."

I said, "Harley, I wonder could we just step outside and have a brief conference."

He said, "Ain't nothing to conference about, mama knowed I sold her house for three thousand dollars she'd swivel in her grave."

I give Mrs. Cartwright a little smile, led Harley out to the porch.

Said, "Harley, the love of money is the root of all evil, them that covets it has erred from the faith and has pierced theirselves with many sorrows. That there's your book of Timothy. Way I look at it, if money is the root of all evil, the more you got the more sorrows is going to pierce you. Course the Lord don't want nobody to be flat ass broke either, says that somewheres else in the scriptures. I figure three thousand dollars ain't enough to bring no sorrows down on us, same time it puts us back on the revival trail."

Harley stood a minute looking away, shook his head, said, "I don't know." Seen he was wavering.

Henry come over there, said, "She make you a offer?"

Harley said, "You might could call it that, three fucking thousand dollars."

I said, "Harley."

Henry said, "Take it, I seen share croppers living in better than this crummy shack."

Done a little more Yell county arm twisting, Harley finally give her up, said, "I just hope mama don't find out what I done."

Mrs. Cartwright wrote us out a check for three thousand, we drove up to the Farmer's Bank, I told Harley to sign the check, that I'd take care of the paper work.

He said, "You're going to put it in my name ain't you?"

I said, "Put it in all our names, mine, yours, and Henry's."

Still had a burr up his ass, Harley did, said, "Damn it, it was my house we sold, mine and mama's. Hell, we ain't knowed Henry but only three or four days, I don't even know what her last name is."

Henry said, "Hesterman."

I said, "Listen to your book of Acts, Harley, says, now the company of them that believed was of one heart and soul, nobody said any of them things he possessed was his own, but they was to hold everything in common . . . ."

Harley said, "I'm bout up to my ass in them scriptures."

I said, "Take Ananias. Sold a piece of property, tried to keep the money for hisself, old Peter heard about it, said, how come satan has filled your heart? Said, you done lied to the Lord and he ain't going to like it. Ananias heard them words, seen that stern look on old Peter's face, he let out a little moan, fell down dead as a stomped snake." Let that soak in a minute, said, "This here ain't your money, Harley, it ain't mine and it ain't Henry's. This here three thousand dollars belongs to the Lord, you and me and Henry is just the poor weak vessels of his mighty plan."

He sit there a little thinking it over, finally said, "All right, but you put my name first."

Went in the Bank, little squinty-eyed woman come over, give us the up and down, asked could she help. Told her what our business was, opened our account with twenty-five hundred dollars, put Harley's name first, kept in hand five hundred for casual expenses.

Went down to the Big Store, bought Henry two dresses, a pair of overhauls, some under britches, bought her and Harley and me new shoes, one of them no-stick frying pans and a fancy apron with purple flowers stitched on it for Aunt Heather.

Went and picked up Aunt Heather, stopped at the commissary procured fifty some odd dollars worth of staples, two cases of Lone Stars, set out for the farm.

Something in my soul a singing, rolling along there about seventy, that batmobile shaking like a dog shitting peach seeds, near bout lost control on the curve below the pole bridge, Henry riding in the back seat with Harley let out a whoop, yelled, "Kick her in the ass!"

Looked at Aunt Heather, seen she'd done gone into a state of paralysis, said, "You all right!"

She said, "Merciful Redeemer!"

Got her up to eighty coming down Penny hill, flank speed with wind and tide, trailing dust and black smoke, heard the right front tire blow, same time felt her lurch and swerve, tried to hold her in the road but couldn't, jumped a ditchful of buckleweed, decapitated a blackjack sprout, come down astraddle the fencerow, took out eight of them oak posts and fifty yards of barbwire, come to a dead stop, dust pouring up through the floorboard, little spiral of blue smoke coming from under the hood.

Nobody said nothing for a minute, Aunt Heather sit there shaking her head slow, said, "It's the Lord's retribution, boy, he's done caught on to your wicked ways."

I looked around, seen Henry and Harley was all right, said, "Ain't nobody hurt, Aunt Heather, the Lord was riding with us."

Henry said, "Was, he ought to have his head examined."

I said, "Now, Henry, we ain't going to have no blaspheming around here."

Got out and raised the hood, seen the smoke was coming from the oil spigot, nothing to fret about, told Harley to get out the spare tire.

He said, "We ain't got no spare tire."

Remembered he'd sold it while on that binge in Caledonia, but wasn't in no mood to brood. Got them back in the car, drove her in on the flat tire. Coming up the wagon lane to the house, for just a minute there caught myself looking for Elijah, the way he'd always bring me a greeting when I'd been off somewheres. Mind works funny.

Got the car unpacked, took our ease on the back porch, drinking beer and counting our many blessings. Aunt Heather come out there with a glass of buttermilk, a fine Christian woman, pure of heart, body and soul, sit there a minute watching Henry swill that Lone Star, said, "Ain't you a little young to be drinking hard spirits?"

Henry said, "Ain't my doing, doctor put me on it. I got this kidney disease, doctor told me to drink three or four beers a day, keep my system flushed out."

Seen Aunt Heather cut her eyes over at me, give my head a shake, went back to tracking dirtdabbers along the ceiling. You got a Henry on your hands, better just to leave the motor running.

Along about sundown Aunt Heather and Henry went to fix some supper, me and Harley wandered off down to the creek. Sit awhile listening to the soft hum of insects, now and then a bass slashing around in the sledgeweed along the bank, a little breeze stirring in the trees. Sounds that brings peace to troubled souls.

Harley said, "You decided yet where we're going to hold our next revival?"

I said, "Dalton."

He said, "Shit, man, that there's a mean town."

Said, "Harley, whither we are called, there we will goeth."

He said, "Ain't nobody calleth me to get my head busted. What we going to do them millhands get juiced up, come making trouble for us?"

Said, "Offer them the sweet peace that passeth understanding. That don't work, smite hell out of them with the jawbone of a ass."

Chapter Six

Monday morning we piled in the batmobile, drove down to Dalton, little over a hundred miles south of Howtown on the Loosahatchie river. Bullet pocked sign at the edge of town said: Pop: 3,246. Turned out about half of them moved in after the sawmill set up out on the river bluff.

Took a little tour down main street, few stores, three slumgullion cafes, counted six beer joints between the Bank and cotton gin at the lower end. Around noon, them beer joints doing a steady business, found out later the sawmill run three eight hour shifts, like the Reverend Dicker said, them that wasn't sawing timber was cahooting with the devil in them main street honkytonks.

After a little Henry said, "This here's a shitty town, ain't it?"

A home truth, garbage piled in the alleyways, rightaway along Main growed up in bitterweed, one of them sprung up towns, full of casual litter and trashy people.

Stopped at the Red Dot cafe, bought a six pack, half a dozen pickled eggs, three snicker bars, drove out the river road towards the mill. River same as the town, low in August, banks strewed with empty cans and food wrappers, still half a mile away you could smell the dead fish and woodrot.

Come to the river bend, road curved back left straight up to the bluff, got up there pulled over to one side, sit awhile looking. Off to the left the Deerfield Mill and Lumber Company Inc. Must a covered two hundred or more acres, them corrugated roofs glittering in the sunlight, bucksaws squealing like a runty sow in labor, logs piled far as you could see in the drag yard.

Something to see, even Henry for a little there was rendered silent, then she said, "How long we going to sit here studying that crummy sawmill?"

Drove on a little ways, stopped under a grove of trees along the river bank and eat our dinner.

Harley said, "We got our next move planned yet?"

Done been thinking about it, said, "Next two moves. First thing we're going to find a place to set up our tent. Next I'm going back to town, make a call on some leading preacher, see can I drum up a little local support for our meeting."

Which is what we done. Mile or so on down we come to a clearing big enough to hold our tent, wasn't fenced off or nothing, figured it was public property, didn't know nobody more public than me and Harley and Henry. Anyhow it beat paying rent to some gizzard-faced old man with a wife in heat and a giveout dick.

Put Harley and Henry to making up posters, Harley said, "How you going to find this here leading preacher?"

I said, "Ask around I reckon."

Henry stood up, didn't say nothing, went walking off towards the river, I said, "Sister Henry, where might you be going?"

She said, "Going to pee, want to come watch?" Went ahead walking.

Harley shook his head, said, "What we going to do with that girl?"

I said, "Abide her, Harley, hope the Lord will someway touch her wayward heart."

Church sit back on a side street three blocks from Main, sign out front, said:

FIRST BAPTIST CHURCH OF DALTON
REVEREND D.D. DICKER, PASTOR

"And when he is come, he will reprove the world
of sin, and of righteousness and judgment"
John 16

Wasn't nobody around, front door open, so I went on in. Thought, I had me a church like this ain't no telling how many lost souls I could bring to the fold. Big room with a pulpit up front, raised platform where the choir sit, door off to the left at the rear. Went back there, seen the door was a little ajar, stood a minute listening, didn't hear nothing, nudged the door on open. A mortal mistake.

Sitting there at a table studying a piece of paper was the Reverend Dicker, sitting next to him a pudgy little woman holding a notebook and pencil. Only thing, her dress was hitched up clean to the firezone and Reverend Dicker's left hand was planted square on the timberline.

Woman jumped up pawing at her dress, turned the other way, stood there staring up at the ceiling, backbone stiff as old Dicker's tallywhacker. Dicker sit a minute trying to pull hisself together, finally said, "That'll be all for now, Mrs. Hurdley, we can finish these notes later."

Mrs. Hurdly come sweeping past me, counting the cracks in the floor, Dicker stood and give me a little nod. One of them thin shouldered, gourd-shaped fellars, all ass and belly.

I held out my hand, said, "I'm Reverend Claude Dee Moran Junior, take it you're Brother Dicker." He give another nod, I said, "I'd bout decided wasn't nobody home, hope I didn't interrupt nothing." Didn't come out exactly right but it was done said.

Old Dicker decided to play it straight, said, "Not atall, not atall, Mrs. Hurdley and I was just working on some sermon notes, nothing pressing." I let that one float, he said, "Mrs. Hurdley works part-time as church secretary, won't let us pay her a penny. She's a saint, that woman."

I said, "Well, they ain't too many of them around." Thought, I done got you by the gonads and we both know it, what you might call your incriminating evidence, looks like I done fell in it and come out smelling like odie cologne.

Said, "Brother Dicker, I'm what you call your roving revivalist, go like Paul of old wherever the Lord sends me, searching for the lost and unsaved. Done some heavy praying after my last meeting, heard the still small voice, said, take up thy tent and go down to Dalton, them preachers down there's doing a fine job but they need help, I want you to just gird up your loins and go ahead on, so that's what I done."

He stood a little, shook his head, said, "I don't know, seems like satan's somehow got a hold on Dalton, maybe can't nobody save it. Used to be a nice, quiet town, place to settle down and raise your kids, then three years ago the mill come in, northern owned, brought in all that riffraff, long haired hippie kids, got no respect for God or country, nothing or nobody, streets at night ain't safe for decent people. Ought to give them all a lye soap bath, good All American haircut, then run them out of town." He stopped, give me a long squinty look, said, "You ain't by chance one of them liberal preachers are you?"

Hadn't give that no serious thought. One thing though, near as I could remember I hadn't never seen no picture of Jesus with short hair. Onliest one had his hair cut was old Sampson, left him so weak he couldn't a screwed a dandelion.

Said, "What I am, Brother Dicker, is what you call your Apostolic Constitutionalist, a position I come to after reading Gullheimer's famous book 'God, Politics, and Satan.'" Just threw that in, didn't want to get caught in a bind. Said, "What that basically is is a man that takes the Lord on faith, the constitution on principle, and the devil as his mortal foe."

He said, "Can't argue with that."

Said, "Way I figure, it ain't my place to give comfort to nobody, excepting maybe helpless little children and old sick women. The rest is fair game, sinners to the core, mean-hearted and dirty-minded. My way of thinking, sinners needs damning, needs to be showed the error of their wicked ways. That's what I do, damn them a little while before they get there, all the time they're there, a little while after they leave. Lead them to the edge of the fiery furnace and ask one simple question, is that there where you want to spend eternity?" Seen I hadn't got him yet, said, "The gospel according to the wages of sin is death, it's all there in the good book, Behold, I was borned in iniquity, and in sin did my mother conceive me. Says, There is none righteous, no, not one, and if we say we have not sinned, we deceive ourself and the truth is not in us."

He didn't say nothing for a little, then said, "You're asking me to help in this revival?"

I said, "No, sir, I ain't. Got my own revival team, songmaster's Brother Harley Biggs, General Coordinator's Sister Henry Hesterman . . . ."

He said, "Sister? You got a woman on your team?"

Said, "Yes, sir, I have, times though, way she thinks and talks, you'd take her for a man." Give him a minute to chew on that, said, "I'll be opening my meeting a week from today, about a mile below the bluff on the river road, what I'm asking you to do is announce it at your Sunday preaching, urge your people to come out and hear some old fashion hardrock preaching."

He was still running cool, said, "Well, I don't know, truth is I don't know nothing about you only what you've told me, I can't make no promises on that."

I said, "Well, I don't want to crowd you. You think about it, just do whatever your heart tells you is right." Counted ten, said, "And next time you see Mrs. Hurdley, give her my kindliest regards."

━━━━━━━━━━━━━━

Later that week, a Wednesday, I think, left Henry nailing the barn back together, me and Harley went up town to Tooter's garage, put new brake linings on the batmobile. Got back to the farm a little after noon, seen sitting in the front yard a green chevy with Texas license plates. Drove around back and parked, went down to the barn, found Henry sitting in the breezeway drinking a can of beer.

Said, "Whose car's that?"

She said, "Some woman, come to see you. Come bout an hour ago, said she knew you before."

I said, "Didn't say what her name was?"

She said, "Didn't say, I didn't ask."

I said, "What'd she look like?"

She said, "Tall, brown hair, pretty if you like them skinny."

Knowed then who it was. Knowed in the depths of my mortal soul, knowed for sure and certain by the turmoil in my beating heart.

I said, "She up at the house?"

She said, "No, said she'd be waiting down by the creek." She give me one of them sideways looks, said, "She somebody you was expecting?"

Said, "I reckon maybe I was."

Went down through the field, wondering what I'd say we come face to face. Things come back, things I'd sometimes thought about when I laid awake up at Pordell. Times I was bitter cause she never wrote, but that was then. Done put all that behind me.

Followed the fencerow down to the willow grove where the creek widened out to a deep pool, place we used to go to late of an afternoon to swim.

Seen her sitting there on the bank, wearing a yellow dress, ribbon tied in her hair. Come up quiet behind her, knowed she knew I was there but she didn't look around.

I said, "You come back."

She threw a stick in the water, sit a little watching the ripples circle out, said, "Yeah, I come back."

I'd forgot the sound of her voice, soft and low. I said, "For good?"

She looked at me, then looked away again. Said, "Don't ask me that, I done made a life for myself somewheres else. I'm back for now, that's all I know."

I said, "Why'd you come back?"

She shook her head, said, "I don't know. Remembering maybe the way things was. Mama wrote me you'd got out, said she seen you up town, that set something off inside me there ain't no way to explain. Like a fever that won't let go." She looked up and smiled, said, "They's things about a man a woman don't forget."

Wasn't nothing said for a little, then she said, "I reckon you can't forgive me what I done."

I said, "Ain't nothing to forgive, it's over and done with."

She said, "You don't hate me?"

I said, "I thought about that, them long nights I was up at Pordell. Figured it all out, hate ain't nothing but some kind of self torment. I done got out of the hating business long time ago."

Quiet again except for the birds singing off in the willows, finally she said, "You want me to tell you why I left?"

I said, "No."

She said, "It wasn't no man, there wasn't nobody else. I just ain't one to wait. I was lonely, that's all."

I said, "Well, everybody gets lonely, one time or another." She was still looking away, off down the creek, I said, "You ain't got no man now?"

Something I didn't have no right to ask and wished I hadn't. She just sit there, spangles of sunlight in her hair, looking off down the creek. Answer enough.

I said, "Well, however it turns out, I'm glad you come back."

She looked at me, smiled a sweet smile, said, "Me too."

We sit awhile longer, talking about one thing and another, sit apart, not even touching. Talked about olden times, buying the farm, how we worked our fingers to the bone trying to make something out of it. Talked about the time we found a blacksnake under our bed, me running off to get my shotgun, time I got back she'd done picked it up and throwed it out the window.

I didn't tell her nothing about the years up at Pordell and she didn't say nothing about where she'd been or who with. Just talked about us, back when life wasn't nothing but love and laughter.

Later went back to the house, found Harley and Henry on the porch shelling peas.

I said, "This here's Miss Henry Hesterman, you know Harley."

Reckon Harley had done told Henry who she was, Henry give her a beady-eyed once over, said, "You come back to stay?"

I said, "Miss Henry."

Ada said, "It's all right." Said to Henry, "I come back, that's all."

Harley went and got Ada's suitcase out of the car, I took Ada to the back bedroom. She went and stood looking out the window, off somewheres else I reckon. First time since I couldn't remember when I thought about that day I come in from squirrel hunting, seen her and Larry Lee laying there on that bed, a mortal desecration. Funny how without no reason your mind goes back looking for misery.

Then Ada said she'd drove half the night, that she needed to sleep awhile, so I left her be and went back out to the porch.

Henry sit cross-legged, staring off across the fields. I said, "Where's Harley at?"

She said, "Down there hammering some more of that barn together."

I said, "Why ain't you helping?"

She didn't say nothing, just sit there a good little while, finally said, "How come you didn't tell me you was married?"

I said, "I didn't see no reason to."

Quiet a little, she said, "She left you?"

I said, "I ain't putting no blame."

She said, "How come she left?"

I said, "Lonely, I reckon. I wasn't here."

She said, "Where was you at?"

I said, "Up at Pordell prison."

She said, "You was in prison?" She wasn't shocked or nothing, wasn't much shocked Henry, more like the idea took getting used to.

I said, "I killed a man."

Maybe a minute wasn't nothing said, she just sit there looking at me, finally said, "How come?"

I said, "It ain't something I care to talk about."

Sit a little longer, Henry looking again at the sunburnt fields. She said, "One thing I know, you killed somebody, you had good reason."

Not true maybe, but I reckon that's what I needed somebody to say.

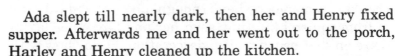

Ada slept till nearly dark, then her and Henry fixed supper. Afterwards me and her went out to the porch, Harley and Henry cleaned up the kitchen.

Sit awhile not talking, finally she said, "You want to walk down to the creek?"

It was a moonlight night, the fields damp with early dew, the trees dim and shadowy against a starlight sky. We went down to the willow grove and laid down amid the memories on the wet grass. There wasn't nothing to say that wouldn't be just words.

Stars spangling the sky, far off the mournful barking of a dog, the hawk of a night bird. A long time we laid there, listening to the night sounds. Finally she turned towards me, touched my face, then I felt her hands move down, fretting with my clothes, her breath warm against my neck, heard her whisper, "Let's make out tonight's forever."

My beloved is mine and I am his, he pastures his flock among the lilies, turn, my beloved, until the day breathes and the shadows flee, be like a gazelle or a young stag upon rugged mountains, behold you are beautiful, my love, you are stately as a palm tree and your breasts are like its clusters . . . .

So for one everlasting night, she come from somewhere and give me back my love.

I woken at dawn, the willow grove still as death. Knowed I was alone, no surprise in that, we're all of us what we are. You don't ask nobody to give what they can't give, or be what they can't be. You've learnt that, you got a headstart on heartbreak.

I stayed down there till the sun was an hour in the sky, listening to the blue jays fretting. Later went back to the house, seen Henry standing on the back porch waiting.

I sit on the back steps, wasn't nothing said for a little, then she said, "I heard her leave, in the middle of the night, come and got her clothes and drove away." I didn't have nothing to say to that, she said, "Maybe she'll come back."

I said, "No, she ain't coming back."

She said, "Well, maybe you're better off without her."

I said, "That could be."

She was quiet a minute, then said, "You want her back, don't you?"

I said, "She ain't mine to want no more." Thought, the harder truth is, I reckon she wasn't never mine to want.

Henry said, "You want a beer?"

I said, "That'd be fine."

Chapter Seven

Sunday afternoon we loaded the tent on the Dodge, drove down to Dalton. Got there around sundown, too late to get nothing done, left Henry down in the clearing to guard the tent, me and Harley drove over to the county line, procured a case of beer and a bottle of drinking whiskey. Stopped in town on the way back, purchased enough supplies to last us the week, six loaves of bread, jar of peanut butter, few cans of hominy grits and collard greens, case of belly washes, and a box of snicker bars.

Got back to the clearing Henry wasn't there, went and found her swimming in the river, naked as a fresh plucked chicken.

I said, "Henry, how you think you're going to guard our tent, you're down here flopping around in this river?"

She said, "I ain't flopping around, I'm taking a bath."

I said, "Another thing, I don't want to catch you down here no more without no clothes on."

She said, "Why?"

I said, "That's why."

She said, "That ain't no reason."

I'd about run out of patience, said, "Reason enough." Said, "What you don't seem to understand is they's all kinds of degenerates running around, what you think's going to happen one of them comes along, catches you down here cavorting around in your birthday suit?"

She said, "I don't know, cause I don't know what a degenerate is."

I said, "It's somebody don't think no more about despoiling a virgin child than he does whistling Dixie."

She said, "He ain't going to despoil no virgin he gets hold of me. I was ten years old, me and Billy Housman . . . ."

I said, "Henry, I don't want to hear no more about it, just get your clothes on and come eat your supper."

Went back to the clearing, heard her down there laughing, thought, what that girl needs is a willow switch laid not too gentle on her scrawny toecus.

Got back up there, Harley said, "You find her?"

Said, "Yeah, I found her. Swimming down there in the river, stripped to her bejesus."

He said, "Ain't nothing wrong with that, I ain't never heard of nobody swimming with their clothes on." Sit there with that idiot grin on his face, said, "You swim with your clothes on?"

Between Henry and Harley I'd had for the time being about all I could take, said, "Tell you what you do, Harley, you open that there jar of peanut butter, start spreading it on that lightbread. It comes in your head to ask another one of them smart-alecky questions, don't take it personal when I kick the mortal shit out of you."

Henry got up there we eat our supper, didn't nobody say nothing much. I could feel them watching me, figuring I reckon I was some kind of Judas. Thought I oughten to a blowed up that way, but where I come out was, to hell with it.

Finished my supper, went down to the river and sit awhile, watching moonbeams dance on the water, listening to the soft drift of the current going on to somewheres. Truth was, I still had Ada on my mind. I kept thinking about us laying down there on the creekbank, her face in moonlight, the way she touched me, things she whispered in my ear. Like Aunt Heather would a said, a fool dancing to a fool's tune, cause I knew deep in my bones I wouldn't never see her again.

After awhile I heard Henry coming down the hill. She come over to where I was, sit down, didn't say nothing for a little, finally said, "I won't swim naked no more, you don't want me to."

I said, "Fine."

Sit a little longer, she said, "Is it all right if I swim in my panties, my chest is flat as a corn fritter, one of them degenerates comes along he ain't going to know if I'm a boy or a girl."

I said, "That'll be fine, Henry."

Must a sit five minutes not saying nothing, she said, "I don't want you to send me away, cause I can't think of no place in the world I'd rather be than with you and Harley."

I said, "Ain't nobody said nothing about sending nobody away."

She said, "You ain't mad?"

I said, "No, I ain't mad."

She give me that crooked grin, said, "You get mad, it scares the hell out of me."

Thought, Henry, they ain't nothing been borned,

spawned, or hatched that scares the hell out of you.

———————

Next morning we went into town, stuck some posters around announcing my sermon for the evening, which was MIRACLES AIN'T NOTHING BUT THE SOUL COME ALIVE. I'd give that quite a little thought.

We done some promoting along main street, talking up our revival, even went in a couple of them honky-tonks where I give a brief prayer, stopped by the Red Rooster and had a bowl of chili, then went on back out to the river.

Back breaking work setting up that tent in the middle of the day, sun beating down with a mortal vengeance, hadn't been at it long Harley had one of them heat strokes of his, eyes rolling up in his head, gasping and gagging like a chicken that's swallowed a buckeye, said he'd sweated out all his fluids so we went and sit under the shade of a tree and drunk a few Lone Stars.

Harley had two or three more heat strokes, it was after six o'clock we finished getting the tent in place. Went down to the river and washed off the sweat and dust, time we got changed into our meeting clothes the first cars was already coming into the clearing. Sent Henry to direct traffic, told Harley to check out the tent, went to a quiet place down the river aways and done some serious meditating.

Come preaching time I went back up there, couldn't hardly believe what I seen, clearing full of cars and trucks, more parked along the road. Looked like old Dicker and Mrs. Hurdley had done a little promoting of their own.

Went inside, must a been a hundred or more people sitting there, men, women, children, a beehive hum of voices, a baby crying in the back, somewheres outside a dog barking. All them sounds one sound to me, the sweet lovesong of glory be.

I come in the voices stopped, onliest sound was the baby crying and the barking dog, felt the thumping of my own heartbeat, a little know taking hold in the pit of my stomach, hadn't felt nothing like that before, never felt nothing like it again.

Went over and took my seat between Harley and Henry, Henry leaned over, said, "We ought to make a killing tonight."

I said, "Sing, Brother Harley."

He leaned over, said, "Me and Henry's going to sing a duet, we been practicing."

Thought, Lordamighty, I done been struck by the wrath of God.

They got up there, song went, "Oh come, loud anthems let us sing, loud thanks to our almighty king." Sung loud all right, Harley in one key, Henry in another. Sounded like two cats rutting in a briar patch. Couldn't bring myself to look at the congregation so studied my shoe laces and done some more meditating.

They got finished I give a short prayer, Harley sung his solo, then I read a little scripture I'd wrote down, went, "Even the sparrow finds a home and the swallow a nest for herself, blessed are the men whose strength is in thee, as they go through the valley of Baca they make it a place of springs, and the early rain covers it with pools. The eye is the lamp of the body, so if your eye is sound your whole body will be full of light, but if your eye is not sound, your whole body will be full of darkness."

Went right into my main sermon, something I'd been thinking about a good little while, talked along there about miracles, the miracle of healing, the miracle of feeding the multitudes, them miracles we hear about, then come to my basic point which I still hold to, that they's other kinds of miracles, that miracles is everywhere, in the sunrise and the sunset, in the sweet faces of wild flowers, in sunlight on still water, the wind in trees, the soft hum of insects on a summers day, snow, rain, sleet, hail, all miracles, that miracles ain't happenings, they're a feeling in the soul, a feeling for whatever's ugly or beautiful or lonely or scared or lost or beat down.

Somebody in the back give me a amen. Went on, "The eye ain't only the lamp of the body, it's the lamp that sees through the darkness, that sees hope where they ain't no hope, that sees in the eyes of little children the sweet light of love . . . ."

Going along like that, then's when it happened. First seen the tent sway a little, them rigger poles listing slightly to one side, wasn't no wind or nothing, took me about a ten count to figure out what was happening. All a sudden knowed for damn sure they was some scutters out there sabotaging my revival, done cut the guy lines and was pulling the tent down. Yelled out for everybody to lay flat on the ground, run for the flap opening but didn't make it. Them rigger poles keeled over collapsing that tent, people started screaming, babies crying, I was yelling "Praise the Lord!" trying I reckon to calm them down. Started crawling towards where I figured the flap opening might be, finally made it outside, about the same time seen Henry come crawling out. We tried pack rolling the tent off them people but wasn't getting nowhere, then three or four men come running up and we taken hold of them loose guy lines, peeled that tent back like you'd take the hide off a fox squirrel. People underneath was still carrying on as we got them uncovered, women huddled over their babies, old folks moaning and calling out to the Lord to save them from devastation, quieted down a little they seen they wasn't dead and buried.

Time we got the tent off and pulled back out of the way, people had done started for their cars. For a minute there I couldn't think what to do or say, finally run up that way, yelling, "Folks, you seen tonight the work of the devil! He's laid us down a challenge and tested our spirits!"

Didn't nobody look back. Said, "Oh, ye of little faith! God is love! Yea, though I walk through the valley of death, I will fear no evil!" Just saying anything that come to mind, but it didn't do no good, they kept on a walking. Reckon I knowed right then, deep in my heart, that my revival business had done gone defunct.

About then Harley and Henry come walking up, Harley said, "You want me to sing a solo, might be that'll bring them back."

I said, "Harley, ain't nothing going to bring them folks back, but if you feel it in your heart to sing, ain't nobody going to stop you."

Me and Henry went back down to the car, left Harley standing there in the fading light singing "Onward Christian soldiers, marching as to war . . . ."

━━━━━━━━━━━━━

Later we went down and sit by the river, a moonlight night, the wind up a little, from somewhere downstream the sweet strains of a harmonica. Drunk a beer or two, nobody said nothing for awhile, knowed they was waiting for me to state my future plans. Truth was I didn't at the moment have no future plans.

Finally Harley said, "Tomorrow we get that tent put back up, I aim to get me some tackle, do a little fishing."

I said, "We ain't going to put no tent back up, we'll load her on the car in the morning, get on back to the farm."

He said, "The farm? What about our revival?"

I said, "Harley, we done held two meetings. First one ended with old man Dickerson threatening to blow my mortal ass to kingdom come, this one ain't halfway through the first sermon, somebody comes out here and swamps our tent. Ain't it crossed your befuddled mind that maybe the Lord is sending us a sign?"

He said, "What's the mean?"

I said, "Means maybe we ain't been called to preach atall. Means maybe when the Lord said, go tend my flock, he was calling us to raise sheep."

He said, "You saying we're getting out of the revival business?"

I said, "That's something I ain't yet figured out."

He said, "You ain't mad, them sonsabitches come out here, scuttled our tent thataway?"

Truth was I wasn't. I didn't have no feelings about it one way or another. Onliest thing I felt right then was a little soul weary. Said, "Mad don't get you nowhere, mad don't burden nobody but your ownself."

About then Henry set in, said, "I ain't believing what I'm hearing, you sitting there talking about going back to the farm like ain't nothing happened, what we ought to do is find out who it was fucked up our meeting, track them scutters down, cut their nuts out and feed them to the hogs . . ."

I said, "Take it easy Henry, it's a long ways from here to sundown."

PART TWO

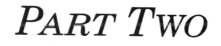

THE LAWMAN

The law is a sort of hocus-pocus science.

Charles Macklin

When constabulary duty's to be done,
The policeman's lot is not a happy one!

William Gilbert

She wasn't no raving beauty, but like Harley once said,
turn out the lights they ain't no bad ones.

Claude Dee Moran Junior

Chapter Eight

We got back to the farm a little after noon the next day, come over the last rise Henry said, "Pretty ain't it?" Talking about them wild flowers we'd planted in the front yard, mostly her doing, all colors and shapes, kind of glittering in the mid-day sunlight.

I said, "Pretty as a mountain meadow, best thing I ever done's put you in charge of our home beautiful program."

Drove a little on, she said, "Makes our house look a little dinky, don't it?"

Couldn't argue with her there, said, "Well, I don't know as dinky's the right word, but I ain't saying it's no Tashmer Hall either."

Turned up the wagon trail, always thought of Elijah when I come back from somewheres, way he'd use to come greet me, Henry said, "How come we don't just give her a paint job?"

Thought about that a minute, couldn't think of no reason not to, said, "Well, we got a few days to get ourselves organized, might be we'll just give that house a good white-washing."

Harley said, "You're talking about your two or three days of hard labor there."

Henry said, "I ain't thinking no white-wash, white-washing's for poor folks."

I said, "I don't know, we paint that house it's going to cut pretty deep in our financial holdings."

Harley said, "Don't look to me we go broke, I ain't got nothing else we can sell."

Henry said, "You listen to Harley, we're going to end up no better than poor white trash."

Parked under the mulberry tree in the backyard, beer had done gone warm but we drunk it anyhow. Sit awhile on the backporch, I said, "What color you got in mind?"

Henry said, "Orange."

I said, "Lordamighty, I ain't never heard of no orange house."

She said, "Don't mean nothing, I reckon they's lots of things you ain't never heard of."

I said, "That's a fact."

Harley said, "Be better we hold off till fall, let the wea-ther cool down some, I have one of them heat strokes I don't never know if it'll be my last."

I said, "When you want to start?"

Henry said, "Tomorrow morning, me and you can drive into town this afternoon and get the paint. Soon as we've had another one of them beers."

Dawdled around out there till late in the day, got to Palmer's hardware a little before closing time, procured a bottle of linseed oil and six buckets of paint. Wasn't exactly orange but close as we could get, a kind of turdmuckle yellow. Went by Tooter's and borrowed some paint brushes, stopped on the way out, bought another case of beer and a block of ice.

Driving along there on the way back, a kind of peaceful feeling over everything, sun hangs for just a minute tangled in the treetops along the creek, then slides sudden down behind the hills, leaving a soft purple glow over the fields.

After a little Henry said, "You thinking about what we're going to do next?"

I said, "Ain't thinking about nothing, got my mind set on idle."

She said, "Reckon you'll go on preaching?"

Said, "I don't reckon I will."

She said, "You was good at it."

I said, "Not good enough. It wasn't going nowheres."

She said, "You said you was called to it by the Lord."

I said, "Well, I ain't atall sure of that now."

Drove on a little ways, she said, "J.D. says they's a man over at Crabtree getting rich running a whorehouse."

Never knowed for certain when she was baiting me and when she wasn't, said, "Henry, I ain't sure if I was called by the Lord to preach, but I sure as hell know I ain't been called to run no whorehouse."

Wasn't nothing said for quite a little while, then she said, "You're about the funniest man I ever met."

━━━━━━━━━━

Next morning we lit in on that house, put Harley to painting the back porch, me and Henry started on the front. Been working maybe a hour, went to check on

Harley, seen him stretched out under the mulberry tree, still as a corpse, thought, Lordamighty, he's done had another one of them heatstrokes.

Ran over there, seen his eyes was closed, said, "Harley!" He opened his eyes, I said, "You all right?"

He said, "Wore out's all."

I said, "Damn it, Harley, we don't all pitch in, we ain't never going to get this house painted."

He said, "Them palpitations come back on me, I think maybe my bile is out of whack."

Ain't but a little of Harley, you got enough. I said, "Well, I'll take it kindly you just get off your ass and start to painting on that porch."

That bestirred him. He said, "Goddam it, everybody gets tired, the Lord hisself rested after his labors."

I said, "Well, he sure as hell worked longer than maybe an hour before he took out."

He got up, brushed hisself off, said, "Trouble with you, Claude Dee, is you ain't got no toleration in your heart." Give his head a sad shake, said, "I reckon the bible don't say nothing about that."

Got back around to the front, Henry said, "How's Harley doing?"

I said, "I don't care to discuss Harley."

She said, "Something put a burr up your ass?"

I said, "Yeah, little girls with foul mouths."

She give me a slant look, said, "You want to know what I think?"

I said, "No."

She said, "I think maybe you take yourself too fucking serious, Brother Claude Dee."

Around noon I could see we was going to run out of paint. We took a break, had a couple of beers and a snicker bar, I left Harley working, drove back into town.

That there's when a Sign was sent to me. And here's my thinking on that. There ain't much point in trying to plan your life cause it's mostly done planned for you, all laid out like a road map, rivers and roads and highways and byways done wrote in. Since giving up revival preaching, I'd give quite a lot of thought to what I aimed to do next, but woken that morning with no more idea what directions I was going than a peach orchard boar. Then, about one o'clock on a Tuesday afternoon, I walked into Palmers Hardware and right there's where the Lord give me the Sign.

I come in, Palmer's boy Jegley was sitting there reading a magazine. Told him I need four buckets of paint, he went out to the storeroom to fetch it, I picked up the magazine. *The Arkansas Lawman's Journal.* Just thumbing through it, waiting for Jegley to get back, come up on a page, said, "Job Opportunities." My eyes was drawed by divine intercession to this: "Wanted, Town Marshal, experience required, salary negotiable. Send Resume to Barton Suggs, P.O. Box 163, Cotterfield, Arkansas."

Wrote that down on a piece of paper, knowed right then sure as they's saints in heaven I'd been called to track down law breakers and bring them to judgement. Meant having to give up my revival career for good, but the way I looked at it, it was the Lord's work either way. Like it says somewheres in there, For until the law was given, they was sin in the world, have no fellowship with them that sins but reprove them.

I couldn't think of nobody had a better chance to reprove them mothers than a officer of the law.

Henry said, "Somebody's done pulled the plug on you, ain't nobody going to hire a ex-con as town marshal."

I said, "Ain't no reason I can think of why they need to

know that."

Harley said, "I don't know, man could get hurt fucking around with them scofflaws."

Henry said, "Scofflaws? What the hell does that mean?"

I said, "That there's just a fancy word for law breakers. Harley's smarter than you think."

She said, "He'd nearly have to be."

Sitting under the mulberry tree, little breeze blowing in from the creek, eating the pickled pig's feet I'd brought back from town and discussing our dim and uncertain future.

Henry said, "I reckon you done got your mind made up?"

I said, "Pretty much. Ain't for me to say, it's the Lord's work."

She said, "I reckon you want me to hit the road."

I said, "I ain't said nothing 'bout you hitting the road. What's got into you?"

She said, "Ain't nothing got into me. I know when I been dealt out, that's all. Do I look like a female deputy sheriff to you?"

Thought, bless her hard little heart, said, "I ain't looking for no deputy sheriff, done got one . . . ."

Harley said, "I don't know . . . ."

I said, "What I need's a Chief Interrogator."

Henry cut her eyes over there, said, "What's a Chief Interrogator do?"

I said, "Well, say somebody's done committed a crime, rape, murder, something pretty serious, but he won't admit he done it. Say we ain't got nothing but circumstantial evidence, so we go bring him in on that. We read him his rights, give him a chance to change his story but he ain't budging. That's when we take him in a back room, dark except just one light in his face. You start grilling him, stay after him till you break his spirit and he confesses he done it. That there's what a Chief Interrogator does."

She sit a minute, thinking about that, finally said, "I could do that. Fact is, sounds like something I'd be good at."

I said, "Yes, mam, that same thought occurred to me."

Harley said, "I don't know, man could get his ass shot off . . . give a choice, I'd ruther be a songmaster."

I said, "Well, you ain't been give a choice, have you, Harley?"

Knowed I wasn't going to get no lawman's job without I had some credentials. Put Harley and Henry back to painting the house, went in the kitchen and wrote out a certificate, saying I'd done completed the Texas State Patrol School in San Anotonio, then wrote a citation, praising me for my undercover work busting up a dope ring in Culbertson County.

Went back out there, called Henry over to one side, said, "I'm putting you in charge till I get back. Keep a eye on Harley, give half a chance he'll take out on you."

She said, "He ain't taking out on me. I done told him we ain't having none of them fuckoff heatstrokes while you're gone."

A natural born pusher, Henry.

Stopped at Caroltown on the way to Cotterfield, went to the Southern Office Machine & Printing Co., Inc., done my business with a Mrs. Delpha Fargo, pudgy little woman with purple eye makeup, give off the not too faint scent of eau de Walgreen's. She give my citations a pretty careful reading, cut her eyes up at me, but didn't ask no questions. Went somewhere in back and printed the citations on them plaque cards, charged me $12.50.

On the way out of town, stopped at Gina's Gift and Novelty Shop, purchased for $1.98 a lawman's badge, had the word "Police" wrote on it, scruffed it up a little with a handful of dirt, pinned it to my shirt and set out for Cotterfield.

Got into town around eleven o'clock, wasn't in no hurry to contact Suggs, drove around maybe half an hour, liked what I seen, quiet, shady back streets, clapboard houses with neat lawns, three churches, school up on a high hill with a sign out front, said: "Blue Darters, State Champs, 1966." Didn't seem like no place overrun with scofflaws.

At the lower end of town, come to a little park set hard against a winding creek. Sit awhile on a picnic bench, watching two kids see-sawing. Eat a snicker bar, got to thinking about Henry, who maybe hadn't never see-sawed in her whole life. Hadn't never done none of them things kids was supposed to do, just growed up like a stalk of buckleweed, taking whatever come her way, without no pissing or moaning. Never asking for nothing she couldn't have, tough as a corncrib rat from trial and tribulation, but underneath it all still just a kid, though she'd done learned things at thirteen they's some folks won't never learn.

Thought I'd have to watch myself, not let myself get too close to a scrawny, foul-mouthed thirteen-year-old girl.

Went back up town, fellow sitting on a bench in front of the drugstore told me I'd find Colonel Suggs, was what he called him, at his office over in the Farmers Bank and Trust building. Was greeted over there by a punkin-assed woman, stated my business, she said, follow her, led me down a hallway to an office in back.

Woman knocked on a door at the end of the hall, opened it and there he sit, Colonel Barton Centennial Suggs, President of the Cotterfield Town Council, an old geezer, eighty, eighty-five years old, shriveled as a frostbit dick.

Woman said, "Man here to see you," and left. Colonel Suggs leaned a little forward, blinked once or twice, said, "How's that?"

I said, "My name's Claude Dee Moran Junior, seen your ad in the *Lawman's Journal,* come to apply for the job as Town Marshal."

He stood up and held out his hand, said, "Colonel Barton Suggs, what can I do for you?"

I shook his hand, raised my voice about three octaves, told him again why I come.

He said, "What the hell you yelling about, boy! I ain't deaf!"

He sit down, started shuffling through some papers on his desk, said, "I don't see no resume on you, Malone."

I said, "Moran." Said, "No, sir I ain't sent no resume. Had to come over here on a business trip anyways, figured it'd be easier I just applied direct."

Put them false documents on his desk, he didn't make no move to look at them. Looked like he'd dropped off there for a minute.

Just trying to keep things moving, I said, "What happened to your last marshal?"

Slow to bestir, he finally said, "How's that?"

I said, "Your last marshal, what happened to him?"

He said, "He died."

I said, "What'd he die of?"

He said, "Shotgun wounds."

Thought, godamighty, said, "Who shot him?"

He said, "Didn't nobody shoot him, shot hisself. Been sick a year or more, some kind of bladder trouble, clogged bowels, other things. Finally wore him down, I reckon." He sit a minute brooding over that, then give me a long look, said, "You had any experience in law enforcement, Malone?"

Said, "Yes, sir, I have. It's all in them documents I put on your desk. Two years special assignment with the country sheriff's department over at Roswell, New Mexico, last eight years with Midland, Texas SWAT team, mostly undercover work."

He give the documents a hasty once over, said, "And might I ask how come you quit them jobs?"

I said, "Yes, sir, you might. That there's a good question. I was borned over in Howtown, growed up there man and boy, come home last week to bury my poor mama. My papa's bedrid with intestional lumbago, ain't no other family, nobody else to give him counsel and comfort. All he's done for me, I can't hardly bring myself to go of somewheres and leave him to shift for hisself. Figure I can get a job close enough so's I can look in on him from time to time, I'll partly repay the lifetime debt I owe him for his love and fatherly devotion."

Got a little carried away, but Colonel Suggs didn't come along. He said, "Sounds like bullshit to me."

I said, "No, sir, I ain't in the bullshitting business. It's the truth, ever last word of it."

He said, "Well, we can't pay no SWAT team wages. Marshal's job pays two hundred a month and whatever you can pick up in speeding fines. I reckon you noticed Highway 62 runs smack through the center of town. Boswell put up a little sign out by the viaduct, maybe you seen it, sits back aways off the road in a little blackjack grove, states the speed limit is fifteen miles a hour. Boswell used to sit down there behind the Mobil station, motor running, catch them fuckers fast as they come over the rise. On a good afternoon, he'd make fifty, sixty dollars."

That didn't sit just right with me, said, "Well, Colonel, I'm a lawman. You folks are looking for some limber dicked gumshoe to come over here and run a speed trap, I reckon you're talking to the wrong man." Give that a minute to take hold, said, "Understand, it ain't only my own services I'm offering. I aim to bring along my whole force."

He said, "Your whole force?"

I said, "Yes, sir, my deputy, Mr. Harley Biggs, you might a read about him, it was in all the newspapers, how he single-handed broke up a ring of car thieves operating along the Mexican border. Miss Henry Hesterman, serves

as my records clerk, got a strong background in admini-
strative penology, also done extensive work in the lie
detector field."

Seen I'd hit a chord, he sit a good little while thinking
that over, finally give his head a shake, said, "I don't know
as we need no three man police force, Cotterfield ain't
never been much more than a piss stop."

Told myself, you got him leaning, leave it with him.
Said, "Well, sir, that ain't for me to say. Like I said, I'm
a lawman, got the record to back it up, I reckon you people
will have to decide what you need over here."

He sit a little longer, said, "Truth is, crime's going up
in Cotterfield same as everwhere else, more of them long
haired drifters coming through town, niggers out on Gat-
lin's ridge getting restless, all that horseshit bout equal
rights." Give me time to cut the deck, said, "What kind
of money we talking about?"

Wanted to leave myself some room to dicker, said, "Six
hundred a month, squad car that'll run, house fit to live
in, big enough for me and my people."

He said, "We got a car, ain't two years old, been sitting
down there at Chester's garage since Boswell shot hisself.
Got a house too, old Baptist parsonage, city bought it
when they built a new one." Shook his head, "Only thing,
Town Council ain't going to spring for no six hundred
dollars." Blinked them rheumy eyes, watching me pretty
close, said, "I do a little serious arm twisting, might come
up with four hundred."

I said, "That there dog won't hunt. Five-fifty, only reason
I'd consider that is so's I can stay close to my sick papa."
Let him think on that a minute, said, "You talk to your
Town Council, let me know what they decide."

I stood up and started for the door. He said, "Town Council does what I tell them." I stopped, turned around. He
sit there tapping his fingers on the desktop, finally said,

"Five hundred, that's high as I go, twice what I figured to pay."

Bout twice what I figured to get, I said, "You got a deal," and we shook on it.

He said, "When can you start to work?"

I said, "Day after tomorrow, give me time to tie up some loose ends."

So there it was, what you call your gentlemen's agreement. Then he opened a desk drawer, took out a bottle of Jack Daniels, couple of mouldy glasses, and we drunk a few toasts. Drunk to the end of crime in Cotterfield, to our dead mamas, the ten commandments, redbone hounds, easy women, some other things I can't remember. Come time for him to show me around town, he was drunk as a cornfield coot. Truth is, I wasn't feeling no serious regrets myself.

Shuffled him out the back door, shakey as a dried out tator vine, got him over to the car. About then a woman come along, seen me wrestling the Colonel around, stood watching a minute, a anxious look on her face, then she come over there, said, "Colonel Suggs, are you all right?"

Colonel give her a blinky look, said, "Go fuck yourself, Cora."

Woman wasn't shocked or nothing, I reckon it wasn't the first time the Colonel had give her leave to fuck herself. I said, "Nothing serious, mam, little touch of ptomaine he picked up somewheres, he'll be all right soon as I get some pepto bismol down him."

Colonel rode shotgun, I done the driving. First went up to Apple Hill, seen the jail, little concrete block building maybe big enough to hold two scofflaws, they was already on intimate terms. Drove back down town, stopped at the Marshal's office, one room shack next to Dudie's Laundromat, nothing inside but a whompered over desk, couple of chairs, wood filing cabinet with a busted drawer. Figured it would look a heap better after Henry give it her woman's touch.

Last thing we done, drove about half a mile out the old Cherry creek road to the house where me and Harley and Henry was going to live. Big oak tree in the front yard, one of them long verandahs with a porch swing at one end, sweet smelling beds of purple flowers running along the walk leading up to the door. Little rundown but I didn't have no complaints. Thought, it sure as hell beats living out of that revival tent.

The Colonel waited while I has a look around, time I got back to the car he'd passed out cold. Drove around awhile trying to talk him awake but it wasn't no use, he'd done found balm in the holy city of Lynchburg. Didn't have no idea where he lived so drove back to where we started from, stretched him out on the front seat, went and got in the batmobile and lit out for home.

Took a detour through Lincoln City, stopped at the war surplus store bought firearms for me and Harley, a .38 caliber police special in one of them fancy tooled holsters for me, a long barreled .22 caliber automatic for Harley.

Got back to the farm just as the sun was going down, come over the last rise couldn't hardly believe what I seen. They'd finished painting the whole front of the house and all but a little corner of the east side. Took on a kind of red glow in the dying sunlight, long shadows stretching across the fields beyond, looked more like a painting than the place I bought for Ada, where me and her worked side by side grubbing blackjack sprouts in the summer's heat, where we made love by moonlight and lamplight till that fatal day I gunned down Larry Lee and Ada went off in search of whatever it was she thought she was looking for.

Drove around back, seen the well porch was finished, Harley and Henry sitting under the mulberry tree having a beer. Went over there, said, "Y'all done good."

Harley said, "Man ain't afraid of a little honest sweat, do about anything he puts his mind to."

Henry said, "We get that job?"

I said, "Start to work day after tomorrow."

Harley said, "We ain't going to do no more preaching?"

Said, "Heard again the still sad voice, Harley, calling us to gird up our loins go into the law business, it's all the Lord's work."

Went over to the car and got the firearms, come back and unwrapped them, handed Harley his .22 automatic. He stood a minute looking at it, seen he wasn't much excited, he said, "How come I ain't got a fancy holster like you?"

I said, "Well, now, you might just want to ponder who's the Town Marshal and who's the main deputy."

Henry said, "You didn't bring me no gun? I sure as hell ain't going in that back room with no criminals lessen I'm armed."

I said, "Sister Henry, I'll be there while you're doing your interrogating, happens it's against the law to carry firearms in this state you ain't twenty-one years old."

She said, "Ain't no problem there, we're the law, I don't reckon we're going to arrest ourselves."

Said, "I'd take it kindly you'd just go get me one of them cold beers."

Harley still standing there, sulled up like a treed possum, said, "I'm supposed to walk around holding this here gun in my hand?"

Said, "No, you ain't, you stick it under your belt like them famous western gunfighters used to do."

He said, "Good way to get my dick shot off."

I said, "Don't worry about it, Harley, man's better off without one."

━━━━━━━━

Next morning it come a hard rain, blowed by high winds. Come up of a sudden over the foothills to the north, got darker and darker as the clouds rolled in low over the ridge, thunder rumbling like empty coal cars moving slow. Couldn't do no work on the house, we sit on the back porch and watched her come on. Down the valley, across the burnt fields, swept in grey sheets, coming down so hard you could feel the earth shaking. One of them late summer storms full of violence and vexation.

Henry said, "Rain's good, ain't it?"

I said, "Rain's fine."

She sit a little, said, "I wonder where J.D.'s at now."

I said, "You ain't never said who J.D. is."

She was quiet awhile, looking off in the distance, said, "He ain't nobody, I made him up." I didn't say nothing to that, she said, "I reckon you think that's pretty silly."

I said, "No, I don't. Made up people is mostly better than real ones."

She said, "Anyways, you can make them what you want. They don't tell you no lies or laugh at you or slap you around."

A home truth. I said, "That's right, ain't no surprises with made up people."

Come out of the blue, Harley said, "Remember when me and you used to fight ever afternoon on the way home from school?"

I said, "Anything special make you think of that, Harley?"

He said, "No, it just come in my mind." Didn't say nothing, he said, "You used to beat the shit out of me, remember?"

Had a strange mind, Harley did. I said, "No, I don't. Also, I don't know how come we're suddenly discussing it."

He said, "Them was good times is all."

I said, "All times is good times after they're over."

Henry said, "All my times ain't all been good times. I ain't never had no better times than I'm having right now."

I said, "That's what I just said."

She said, "Ain't what I heard you say. You want to know the truth, I don't think you said nothing."

I said, "Well, just might be you ain't studied enough philosophy to get my drift." She sit giving me that slanty look, I said, "That there's your basic Plato, one of them writers I read up at Pordell, said the past ain't over till it's over, the future ain't here till it gets here, so all you got to work with is the present. Called your theory of Reverse Dissemination."

Harley said, "Sounds right to me."

Henry said, "Horseshit."

Bout two hours later the rain stopped, clouds begin to break up, heat waves come up from the fields you could see with your naked eye. House too wet to paint, Henry went off in search of wild flowers, Harley said for some reason he was woreout, went to take a nap, I decided to drive into town and have a visit with my Aunt Heather.

Found her in the kitchen making hogshead mush, went and give her a little hug, thought she looked a mite peaked, said, "You all right?"

She said, "Why wouldn't I be?"

I said, "Looks like I got here in time for dinner."

She said, "You was always good at that."

Sit a little watching her, said the truth, said, "I been missing you."

She said, "Rot."

I said, "Been meaning to come see you but I been so busy I ain't had time to pick a peach." She didn't say nothing, I said, "Wanted to tell you, I give up my preaching."

She said, "Well, I reckon the Lord's sore grieved about that."

Let that pass, said, "Truth is, way things been going I ain't atall sure me and the Lord's been on the same wave length. Seems like everything I done went wrong, had a misunderstanding with a fellar over at Caledonia, he

taken a shotgun to me, moved over to Dalton, drunken millhands pulled down my tent with me and the congregation
in it, figured maybe the Lord was sending me a message."

She said, "Most likely telling you to mend your wicked
ways."

I said, "No, mam, he's done give me another call, said
go into the land and chase down criminals. You're looking
at the Town Marshal of Cotterfield, Arkansas."

She give me a befuddled look, said, "People in Cotterfield hired a convict to be Town Marshal?"

I said, "Ain't a convict no more, Aunt Heather, done
reformed my ways, got my eye on the sparrow. Didn't tell
nobody I done time, didn't nobody ask."

She said, "Claude Dee, they give out brains you must
a been somewheres else, chasing criminals is a mean
business."

I said, "I ain't afraid of no criminals, heard the angel
of the Lord, said, The Lord is with thee, mighty man of
valour. Heard the voice of the Lord, said, Who will I send
and who will go? Said, Here am I, Lord, send me. Book
of Kings."

She said, "Mighty man of valour, is it? You was always
scared of your own shadow, slept with a light on till you
was a growed boy."

I said, "That was then, this is now. Ain't scared no more.
Courage ain't something you're borned with, it's something you come to."

She said, "Only thing you'll come to is old age and a
mess of grief. Harley and that snippety girl, they still
with you?"

I said, "Yes, mam, near about family now."

She said, "I ain't worried about Harley, the Lord looks
after the addled and ailing, but that girl ain't as abiding
as she lets on to be. Comes the time she needs you, you
be there."

I said, "Yes, mam, I will."

She said, "Sit."

Put on the table some of that hogshead mush, hominy grits, collard greens, warmed over crackling bread, beat to hell and gone all them sody pops and snicker bars I'd been subsisting on.

She got up to get more crackling bread, seen a pinched look on her face, she stood a minute holding onto the chair, I went and took hold of her arms, said, "Aunt Heather, your color ain't good, you sure you're all right?"

She said, "Ain't nothing but a touch of indigestion, this heat don't help none." Said, "I'm fine now, sit."

After we'd eat we went and sit on the back porch awhile, talking like we always done about olden times when whe was a pretty lady and I was kid of a boy. Got ready to leave, asked her to go out to the farm with me but she wouldn't, said she had some canning to do, left me somewheres between going or staying. I said, "Aunt Heather, I'd feel a lot better you went to see a doctor, maybe get some pills for that indigestion."

She said, "Stop your pestering, boy, I ain't been to a doctor in twenty years, don't aim to start now."

That woman. I said, "Well, you look after yourself, I don't want nothing to happen to you."

She said, "Ain't nothing going to happen to me, look after your ownself."

Got back home middle of the afternoon, Harley was still napping, Henry planting yellow flowers in the front yard. Parked in back, went around there, stood awhile watching her, she said, "Pretty, ain't they?"

I said, "Pretty as a baby's smile."

She said, "Plants good, the ground wet." Didn't say nothing for a minute, said, "You see Aunt Heather?"

I said, "Had dinner with her."

She said, "How is she?"

I said, "Getting old, seems like she's aged ten years since I come home."

She said, "Ain't nothing you can do about that." Went ahead with her planting, said, "She's a good woman, ain't she?"

I said, "Good as a woman gets."

She looked up, give me a sweet smile, said, "Everbody needs a Aunt Heather."

━━━━━━━━

Next morning we loaded up the batmobile, things we'd need to sit up housekeeping, drove over to Cotterfield. First went to see Colonel Suggs, let him know me and my force had arrived and was official on duty. He give me Boswell's badge, said he didn't have none for Harley, give me the keys to the police car.

I got back out there Harley seen my badge, said, "You ain't got no badge for me?"

I said, "We'll have to send off for you one, they ain't never had no deputy before."

Henry said, "Get me some shears and a tin can, I'll make you one."

Harley wasn't thinking no tin can, said, "How people going to know I'm the law, they don't see no badge?"

I said, "Way you carry yourself, Harley. Lawmen's got a certain way of walking, toes turned in like a stalking panther. We get out to the house I'll show you." Said, "Anyhow, you'll have that pistol jammed in your britches, that right there'll tell people you're the law."

He said, "Maybe will, maybe won't. It ain't the same as having a badge."

Seen he was going into one of his possum sulls, thought, Lordamighty, it ain't enough they's cold blooded criminals out there I got to track down and bring to justice, I also got to put up with a growed man still in the grips of puberty.

Said, "Harley, it ain't no badge going to make you a feared lawman. What's going to carry you through the trials and travails of what we been called to do is something I seen in you many a time. I'm talking the strength and raw courage of a mountain lion."

He sit a minute looking off in the other direction, said, "Well, I ain't scared of nobody, that's what you mean."

I said, "That there's exactly what I mean, Harley."

Thought come judgment day the Lord might want to question me about that one. Dropped Henry off at the marshal's office, put her to cleaning and fixing, me and Harley drove down to Chester's garage to pick up the police car. Seen her sitting there under a leanto shed, one of them low-slung jobs, bright red, the word POLICE painted on the door.

Thought Harley was going to pee in his pants, he said, "Godamighty, you reckon that's our car?"

I said, "That's what I reckon."

Went over there and got out, Chester come walking up, greasy stringbean of a boy, dirty ropey hair hanging down to his shoulders, three day growth of beard, looked like he's just come back from deer camp.

I done some introductions, Chester said, "Colonel Suggs has been telling around you was a famous lawman out west."

Said, "Well, I don't know as famous is the word, I reckon they was a few people knew my face and name."

Harley said, "Out west?"

I said, "Harley, we got work to do out at the house."

He said, "You want me to drive the police car?"

I said, "Be fine, just follow me."

Got out there Harley had another surprise, way he carried on he seen that house you'd a thought we was moving into the Governor's mansion. Had three bedrooms, a kitchen near big as our living room at the farm, a bathroom with a bo-peep shower curtain and a fast-flushing commode.

Worked most of the afternoon getting her in shape, about four o'clock I buckled on my pistol, told Harley I was going back up town and check on Henry.

He said, "You ain't yet showed me how it is I'm supposed to walk."

So I done that. Walked back and forth a couple of times, toes pointed a little in, shoulders kind of slumped, eyes a little narrowed. Told him to try it. Course he overdone it, pigeon-toed and slit-eyed, hunkered over like one of them Choctaws sneaking up on a wagon train.

He circled the room a couple of times, said, "That it?"

I said, "You got it, Harley, what you call your lawman's tread. Tell you one thing, badge or no badge, ain't nobody going to miss take you for what you are."

Put Harley to cleaning the back porch, went on up town. Driving slow along main street, seen people giving me the once over, two or three of them raised a hand in greeting, thought maybe after all my comings and goings, bad times and good, I had at last got to be one of them somebodys.

Drove to the lower end of town, parked by the playground, seen aways off two skin-headed boys, looked like playing with a cat. Sit a little watching, then seen one of them throw the tag end of a rope over the crossbar of the swingset, it come to me of a sudden, thought, Lord-amighty, them damn fool boys is about to string up that cat. Jumped out of the car and run over there, seen that poor cat twisting and turning, bug-eyed as a snared rabbit, pink tip of its tongue sticking out its mouth, yanked the rope out of the boy's hand and let the cat down easy. Went to turn it loose it bit me twice fore I could get it untied. Thought, I reckon, I was out to do it more harm. Seen it was free, stood unsteady a minute getting its bearings, then let out a squeal and went skittering off across the playground.

I stood up and looked at the kid that done the hanging, mean eyed little scutter, face hard as a hickernut, lips pressed together tight as the blade of a closed knife.

Give myself a minute to cool down, didn't aim to lay hands on that boy, said, "What's your name, son?" He didn't say nothing, I said, "That cat ever done you any harm?" Still didn't say nothing, said, "Cat's got feelings, same as me and you, I don't reckon you thought of that." Seen I wasn't getting nowhere, said, "I'm the new marshal of this town and I aim to keep a close watch on you boys, I catch either one of you in this park the next two weeks I'm taking you in, you got that?"

Kid behind me said, "My name's Billy, he's Jody."

Turned and give him a devastating look, said, "Billy what?"

He said, "Billy, sir."

I said, "I ain't talking no sir, what's your last name?"

He said, "Bascomb."

I said, "All right, Billy Bascomb, I want you to tell your mama and papa that Marshal Moran has put this park off limits to you boys for two weeks, also tell them how come I done it."

He said, "Yes, sir."

Didn't seem to be nothing else needed saying so I went and got in the car and drove back up town to the marshal's office. Henry was standing at the door, I come up she said, "How come you're walking like that?"

I said, "Walking like what?"

She said, "Hunkered over thataway, looks like you're down in your back."

I said, "Well, you have to know, I strained my back picking up some boxes out at the house this afternoon, it ain't nothing you need worry yourself about."

She said, "I ain't worried, looks funny's all." Said, "That there fancy car ours?"

I said, "Yes, mam, it is."

She said, "You going to teach me to drive?"

I said, "No, mam, I ain't."

She said, "Don't make no difference, Harley will."

One thing, she'd done straightened out that office, had went to the laundromat next door and borrowed hammer and nails, fixed the desk and filing cabinet, swept and dusted, had that place shining like a courthouse restroom.

I said, "You done worked your woman's magic on this office."

She said, "I ain't finished yet. Be nice we had some pretty flowers to put on that cabinet, wouldn't it?"

I said, "It would."

About then she saw the blood on my hand where that cat got me, said, "What happened to your hand?"

I said, "Got bit by a cat."

She give me a foxy look, said, "Sounds like one of them made up stories." Waited a minute, said, "You want me to ask you another question?"

I said, "Don't make me no difference."

She said, "Well, then, I reckon I won't."

Funny girl, Henry, times I couldn't catch *her* drift.

———————————

Around noon the next day me and Henry was sitting in the office playing checkers, game score Henry seven, me nothing, Harley was out patrolling the city, seen a fellow drive up out front, sit there a couple of minutes sizing things up, then got out and come in.

Big man, had a red beard and a tar barrel belly, stood a minute scowling, said, "You the new marshal?"

I said, "Yes, sir, I am."

He said, "You tell my boys they can't play in the public park?"

Seen he was in a hairy mood, thought, either meet fire with fire, or go at him cagey. Settled on fire.

Stood up, took a hitch at my gun belt, said, "Might you be Mr. Bascomb?"

He said, "That's right."

I said, "Then I reckon it was your boys I banned from the park."

He said, "Ain't no goddam marshal or nobody else telling my boys where they can play and where they can't."

I said, "Well, now it's done done, ain't it. I catch them boys down there anytime the next two weeks I'm hauling their little asses in." Watched his eyes, seen he was a little uncertain what to do next, I said, "Them boys tell you what they done?"

He said, "Said they done nothing. Said they was playing with a stray cat, you come along and told them to stay out of the park."

I said, "What they done's hang that cat."

Henry said, "They hung a cat!"

I said, "Would of, I hadn't come along and turned it loose."

Bascomb said, "I don't know nothin bout no fucking cat, what I do know is you ain't got no right to tell my boys they can't play in the public park, that there's what I told them."

I said, "Witness Mr. Bascomb's last remark, Miss Hesterman." Said to Bascomb, "What you just done's make yourself an accessory to the crime. I catch them kids in that park I'm coming looking for you, throw you in that hotbox up on the hill, charged with constabulary insubordination. That there's a felony."

Henry said, "Throw his ass out of here."

I said, "I'll handle this, Miss Hesterman." Fixed Bascomb with a steely stare, seen his eyes waver, said, "I was you, fore I done anything else I'd drive down there and check that park, be sure them kids ain't there, cause soon as my deputy gets back with my squad car I'll be checking my ownself. Lessen your mama raised a mortal fool you'll get my drift."

He stood a minute trying to muster courage enough to carry it on, run out of time, said, "That there's the way you run this office, you'll be run out of town fore you get good started."

I said, "That could be, Mr. Bascomb, don't nothing last forever."

After he'd left Henry sit looking at me, give her head a shake, said, "What would you a done he'd a jumped you?"

I said, "Shot him down like a rabid dog." Give her a straight face, she said, "Save that bullshit for old dumb Harley." Started setting up the checkerboard, said, "Your play."

Waan't nothing said for a little, she said, "You done right."

I said, "How's that?"

She said, "Dicking old Bascomb around thataway. Sooner people in this town is scared of you, the better off you're going to be."

Something out of my Pordell days come back to me, I said, "That's what Machovilli says, fellar wrote one of them books I read I was in prison."

She said, "I don't know nothing about no Machovilli, what I'm saying is you're either going to be the law, or you're going to be everbody's friend, you sure as hell ain't going to be both."

I said, "That might be, onliest thing, bullying people goes against my nature. Aunt Heather always said I was a tender-hearted boy."

She give me a squirrely look, said, "You got a jump, you don't pay attention to what you're doing you ain't never going to win a game."

Chapter Nine

One morning me and Henry was sitting in the office carrying on that non-stop checkers tournament, game score Henry about a hundred, me maybe five, she said, "This here's a boring job, ain't it?"

I said, "And what brought that on, Sister Henry?"

She said, "We been here nearly three weeks, ain't arrested nobody yet." Jumped a couple of my men, said, "How am I going to be Chief Interrogator, they ain't nobody to interrogate?"

Truth was, we hadn't had no chance to do much reproving. Family squabble down at the mudflats, break up a scuffle or two out at the Red Rooster, take old man Huckabee home when he come up town on a pisser, raising hell with everbody he run into. Nothing serious, seemed like it was Harley had all the close calls.

I said, "Ain't nobody done nothing would give me cause to arrest them, I can't just go pulling people in so's you can practice your interrogation."

She said, "Can't you arrest somebody on suspicion?"

I said, "Suspicion of what?"

She said, "I don't know, suspicion they broke into Fout's drugstore."

I said, "Well now, only thing wrong with that is Fout's drugstore ain't been broke into."

She sit a minute studying her next move, said, "I liked it better we was preaching."

About then Harley come in, had that John Wayne look on his face, said, "Had a nasty one down at Farnsworth's while ago, one of them touchy situations, hadn't a been handled right could a blowed up in my face, looked for a minute there like I might have to call for a backup."

Stood there waiting for me to take him up, I said, "What was that, Harley?"

He said, "I walked in, Farnsworth was into it with this fellar, name of Willigan I think it was, big scutter, must a weighed three hundred pounds, cussing and raising hell, something about Farnsworth selling him some spoilt cottonseed." Waited again but nobody said nothing, he said, "Good thing I come along when I did, good chance somebody could a got killed."

Stopped again, I waited him out a little, said, "How'd you handle it, Harley?"

He said, "Time I got back there Willigan had Farnsworth up against the harness rack, his fist drawed back, other hand holding on to Farnsworth's shirt, I said, hold it right there, big man, he wheeled around, seen he'd been drinking, said, you want some of it asshole? Right then's when I whipped out my firearm, taken dead aim on his belt buckle, said, don't fuck with me, mister, you're talking to the law. That done it, he wilted like a thumped pecker, backed off said he didn't want no trouble with the law, said something else about Farnsworth selling him some bad cottonseed. I said, I was you I'd walk out that door, keep on walking till I come to my senses, cause next time I catch you making trouble in this town I'm throwing your fat ass in the hotbox. He seen I meant business, didn't wait for no grass to grow under his feet, touch and go there for awhile though."

He stood there a minute, waiting I reckon for somebody to give him the crow degerre, said, "After he left, Farnsworth tried to give me a pop and a candy bar but I wouldn't take it, figured it wouldn't look right, me being a law officer."

Nothing was said for a little, seen I wasn't going to win that checker game, I said, "It didn't cross your mind maybe Farnsworth did sell him some bad cottonseed?"

He said, "Course it did, that's why I ask Farnsworth?"

I said, "And what did Farnsworth say?"

He said, "Said it wasn't so."

I said, "And that was good enough for you?"

He said, "Farnsworth didn't have no reason to lie about it." Seen his bottom lip drooping, he said, "Goddam it, I'm out there putting my life on the line, never knowing from one day to another if I'll be dead or alive tomorrow, you're sitting up here playing checkers with Henry, waiting to jump my ass over something I didn't do that don't mean nothing anyhow."

A mighty weariness come over my soul. Thought maybe he was right. Thought, somewheres out there they's birds singing, soft breezes rustling the leaves of trees, slant sunlight making gold shimmers on still waters.

I said, "All right, give Henry the details, she can write up a report, case this one comes back on us."

Got up and put on my hat, said, "I got some things needs looking after, I'll be back in awhile."

I was going out the door, heard Henry say, "You should a brought them mother-fuckers up here, I'd a got the truth out of them."

Thought what it says in the book of Genesis, This is the child which God has graciously give thy servant.

———

First big case come up not long after that, on a Sunday, one of them dark, dismal days that sours the soul, rising wind carrying from far off the smell of rain on dusty fields, now and then a rumble of thunder along the ridges north of town.

Henry was off somewheres riding shotgun with Harley, I was in the office making out the monthly reports, seen a pickup stop out front, man got out and come in. One of them weather-warped fellars, stooped with age and shriveled by time, didn't seem excited or nothing, took off his hat, said, "You the marshal?"

I said, "Yes, sir, I am."

He said, "My name's Hatley, Raymond Hatley, live about six miles out the old mill road, come to report a shooting."

I said, "Yes, sir, you seen a shooting?"

He said, "Heard it."

I said, "And who was it done the shooting?"

He said, "I can't rightly say if it was him or her."

Just stood there, like he'd done had his say, thought, Lordamercy, I need Sister Henry here to interrogate this old fart.

I said, "And who might him and her be?"

He said, "The Berotellis, can't call their first names, moved in about a year ago, foreigners, Bohemian some folks say, close, stays to theirselves, live a mile down the road from my place."

Waited a little but he didn't say nothing more, I said, "I wonder, Mr. Hatley, could you just tell me exactly what it was you seen or heard."

He said, "Come by there a little while ago on my way to town, heard two shots, rifle, sounded like they come from behind the house, didn't see nobody, didn't stop to inquire."

I said, "Well now, that could a been somebody shooting squirrels, or maybe a chicken hawk, couldn't it?"

He said, "Ain't no squirrels around there, they ain't got no chickens, no, sir, it's a human shooting you got on your hands, marshal." He shook his head, said, "I ain't surprised, been expecting something like this to happen, them two fought like rutting sheep, drive by there hear them cussing each other, once seen him chasing her around the house with a ax, shiftless white trash is all they is, both dead it'll be good riddance."

I said, "They got any kids?"

He said, "A boy, bout ten years old, crazy as a coot, hears a car coming, runs out to the road, yanks out his dick and starts jacking-off, it's got so bad some of the women out there comes to town by the Jackson Hill road, four or five miles out of the way. Preacher from Centerville went down there to complain, Berotelli run him off with a shotgun." Shook his head again, said, "I tell you, marshal, them folks ain't even civilized."

I said, "Well, I reckon that's all the information I need, you'll just give me directions, I'll drive down there and check it out."

Didn't have no idea where Harley and Henry was at, so got in the batmobile and set off down the old mill road. Hadn't drove far when I seen the rain coming, sweeping across the fields in layered sheets, hit me with the force of a typhoon, raining so hard I couldn't see nothing, had to pull off the road and wait till it slacked up.

A little after noon when I come to the barn with the Garret Snuff sign painted on the side, Hatley said Berotelli's place was the first house on the left after the barn. Another half mile I seen it, sitting back off the road a hundred yards in a grove of pines, house weather-washed and leaning a little to one side, the front porch roof sagging. Eased the car along a muddy wagon trail, stopped out front and sit a little watching, yard littered, hulk of a wrecked car off to one side, didn't see nobody, didn't hear nothing, rain still coming down but just in a drizzle.

Got out and walked slow around to the back of the house, seen the body laying there, face up, mouth a little open. Standing ten feet off to the side was Berotelli's kid, pinch-faced boy with weazily eyes, just standing there in the drizzle, hair plastered to his head, looking without no feeling I could see at his dead papa. Went over to Berotelli, seen that half his jaw was blowed away, knowed it had to be a high-powered rifle done that, knelt and felt for a pulse, knowing already he was dead as Hogan's goat.

Got up and give the boy a steady look, said, "Your mama here?"

He didn't say nothing, just stood there looking at me, his face blank as a barn wall, I said, "Cat got your tongue, boy?" Still didn't say nothing, I said, "You know who done this?"

Seen I wasn't making no headway, said, "All right, boy, don't go off nowheres, might be I'll want to question you again." Don't know where the hell I thought he was going off to, but that's the way it come out. Stood a minute looking at him, thinking about what Hatley said, "Another thing, I don't want to hear no more bout you beating your taliwacker out there by the side of the road, you can't leave it alone, least you can do is go to the corn crib."

Went up on the back porch and knocked, didn't hear nothing, the door was open, went inside and stood a minute listening, heard somewheres in the back the buzz of a fan, made my way careful down a hallway, come to an open door, seen laying there on the bed eating potato chips and reading one of them nudie magazines Mrs. Daphne Berotelli. Dark-haired, fair-skinned, belly flat as a pancake griddle, one of them nubile forty year olds, wearing nothing but a dirty pink slip with a tear up one side. Wasn't no raving beauty, but like Harley once said, turn out the lights, they ain't no bad ones.

Must a knowed I was there but didn't look up, I said, "Mrs. Berotelli?" Went on reading, stuffing them potato chips down, I said, "I'm the marshal over at Cotterfield." Still didn't get no rise out of her, said, "I reckon you know Mr. Berotelli's laying out there in the back yard."

She laid the magazine down, give me a cool look, said, "Mr. Berotelli's been feeling poorly lately."

I said, "Well, he ain't feeling poorly no more, cause somebody seen fit to dispatch him."

She said, "Dispatch?"

I said, "Yes,mam, shot in the head with a high-powered rifle."

She said casual, "Dead, I reckon?"

I said, "As hog's head mush, but I figure that ain't no surprise to you."

She said, "You thinking I done it?"

I said, "Well, I ain't yet made no official determination, but I'd have to say you're one of my primest suspects."

She said, "Well, what I say is you better find you another suspect, cause I don't know nothing about how Mr. Berotelli got dispatched."

About then she pulled her knees up against her chest, let her slip fall away giving me leave to gaze upon her fruited plains, said, "Let's me and you not worry too much

about Mr. Berotelli right now cause he ain't worth worry-
ing about, wasn't nothing but a mean-hearted man with
a weary dick."

Thought, Lordy, Lordy, here we go.

She sit looking at me with them agate eyes, said, "You
ever read Macho Man?"

Felt a twitch in my groin, thought, hold up there, boy,
this here's a murder case, ain't no time to lose control,
said, "Well now, mam, that ain't got nothing to do with
why I'm here, so just let me ask you this . . . ."

Wasn't no stopping her, she said, "What I was reading
when you come in, this woman said her and her boyfriend
once screwed on a elevator . . . ."

I said, "What I hear, you and Mr. Berotelli didn't get
along . . . ."

She said, "Woman said there was some people on the
elevator, said they never knowed she was getting screwed,
don't make sense does it?"

That done it, figured I didn't right then do my duty, I
wouldn't never do it. Said, "I wonder would you kindly
get some clothes on, Mrs. Berotelli, I'm going to have to
take you in."

She give me a look took the acid out of my battery, said,
"Maybe you're one of them queers, don't care nothing for
women."

I said, "No, mam, I ain't, little strange some folks say,
but ain't nobody ever called me queer."

She jumped off the bed, yanked on a dress, got her shoes
out of the closet, seen I'd took out my handcuffs, said,
"You going to put them things on me?"

I said, "Yes, mam, I am, cause I don't want you running
off while I'm trying to locate the rifle that dispatched Mr.
Berotelli."

Got her cuffed, made her come along while I looked,
found in the kitchen a 30-30 marlin, picked it up careful
by the trigger guard, led Mrs. Berotelli outside.

Seen the boy standing just where he was when I went inside, Mrs. Berotelli looked over at Mr. Berotelli's deceased body, didn't show no feelings atall, called out to the boy, "See you get that cow milked fore dark."

Put Mrs. Berotelli in the car and drove away, went a little ways without talking, rain coming down hard again, finally Mrs. Berotelli said, "I done it in self defense, I done had enough."

I didn't make no reply to that, figured we'd get a wrote out confession back in town, drove a little on, she said, "You'd a screwed me back there, I wouldn't a told nobody about it."

Felt kind of sorry for her, only thing it didn't come out the way I meant it to, said, "Well, mam, I've screwed a lot worse."

Time we got back to town rain had let up some, Harley and Henry was waiting at the office. Took Mrs. Berotelli inside, Henry, mad as a scalded dog, said, "Where the hell you been? Me and Harley's been looking all over town for you."

I said, "An emergency come up, I didn't have no time to run you and Harley down."

She said, "Emergency's ass, you could a left us a note." Give Mrs. Berotelli the once over, said, "Who's this floozie?"

I said, "This here's Mrs. Daphne Berotelli, apprehended for the crime of murder."

Henry said, "Who was it she murdered?"

I said, "Mr. Berotelli."

She pulled me to one side, whispered, "You want me to interrogate her?"

I said, "Ain't nothing to interrogate, she's done confessed to the crime."

She said, "Don't mean nothing. Might be somebody else done it, Mrs. Berotelli's covering up."

Hadn't thought about that, come to my mind that pecker-happy boy could a done it, maybe somebody else hadn't as yet come into the picture.

I said, "Harley, just keep an eye on the suspect while me and Miss Hesterman have a private word."

We went out to the front porch, I told her what happened down there, about finding Berotelli dead in the back yard, about the kid, what Mrs. Berotelli said when I apprehended her.

We went back inside I sent Harley to tell the coroner where he'd find the body, mainly wanting to get him out of the way, said to Mrs. Berotelli, "I wonder would you just take a seat there, they's a couple of questions we want to ask you."

She sit down, Henry went around and sit behind the desk, took a pencil and tablet out of the drawer, didn't say nothing for maybe five minutes, just sit there staring hard at Mrs. Berotelli, finally wrote down something on the tablet, said to Mrs. Berotelli, "Let me say right off I ain't got time to fuck around with you, I seen a thousand of your kind in my time, all the same, lowdown stinking liars . . . ."

I said, "Miss Henry . . . ."

Mrs. Berotelli give me a look, said, "What the hell is this, I ain't talking to no shitass kid . . . ."

Henry was already half out of her seat, I said, "Just a minute, Miss Henry." Said to Mrs. Berotelli, "This here's Miss Hesterman, she's my Chief Interrogator . . . ."

Mrs. Berotelli said, "Chief Screwball, you ask me . . . ."

Fore I could stop her Henry come around that desk like she'd been shot out of a gun, grabbed hold of Mrs. Berotelli's hair, her still handcuffed, started yanking her ever which way, calling her things I hadn't never heard of.

I got over there, pried Henry loose, pulled her off to one side, lowered my voice, said, "Now try to get hold of yourself, Sister Henry." Give her a couple of minutes to cool down, said, "We'll just call off the interrogation for the time being, why don't you step outside and get a breath of fresh air."

She stood a minute, them teeth clamped tight together, finally said, "I don't need no fresh air. I'm all right now, I just don't like people calling me a screwball."

I tried to get things back on track, said, "Mrs. Berotelli, I reckon that's all the questions we got at this time, I'll just write out a confession, let you sign it . . . ."

She said, "I ain't signing nothing."

Looked like maybe Henry had done interrogated us out of a confession, said, "Well now, you done told me it was you shot and killed Mr. Berotelli."

She said, "I didn't say nothing about killing nobody, what I said was I didn't know nothing about it."

Seen things was falling apart, truth was at that point I didn't rightly know what to do with Mrs. Berotelli. Give that a little thought, couldn't think of nothing else to do, said, "Well, mam, I'll just drive you over to Ridgeville, turn you over to the county sheriff."

Which is what I done, which is when I found out I'd fairly fucked up my first big case.

Got to Ridgeville around two o'clock, went to the courthouse and got directed to the sheriff's office. Hadn't never met him before, didn't look like no county sheriff to me, scraggily little fellar name of Fardwell, wearing a moth-eat suit and tie, thin puckered face, loose skin hanging down like wattles on a rooster.

Told him who I was, said, "I brought you a prisoner."

He looked at Mrs. Berotelli, back at me, said, "What's the charge?"

I said, "This here's your murder in the first degree."

He sit a minute tapping his finger on the desk, then pushed a button, a minute later one of his deputies come in, he said, "Put this prisoner in number six."

After they'd went, he said, "You got your report, Marshal?"

I said, "I ain't had time to write no report, I just picked her up a couple of hours ago." Seen a look come on his face I didn't much like, said, "I can tell you anything you want to know."

He said, "You call the county investigator?"

Truth was, I didn't know nothing about no county investigator, said, "That's what I aimed to do soon as I leave here."

He give his head a shake, sucked on his back tooth, said, "All right, what happened."

So I told him, even told him about that sexual bribe Mrs. Berotelli tried to lay on me, got through he said, "You read Mrs. Berotelli her rights fore you asked her any questions?"

Lordamighty. Said, "Hell, she shot her husband, I'd say she ain't got no rights."

He sit shaking his head slow, back and forth, like he'd done run into the village idiot, finally said, "She said she done it, then said she didn't, that right?"

I said, "That's right."

He said, "So that would be your word against hers, wouldn't it?"

I said, "I reckon it would, onliest thing, I'm the law."

He said, "The body, where's it at?"

Said, "I sent the coroner out to get it."

He leaned back in his chair, sit a good little while looking up at the ceiling, said, "Marshal, I'm going to ask you to get me a written report by tomorrow, be shoveling shit against the tide but we got to start somewheres. What you done is break ever rule in the book, didn't read Mrs. Berotelli her rights, didn't do no real investigating at the scene of the crime, didn't notify the county investigator, didn't get no information we can use from the suspect.

Prosecuting Attorney gets this case he's going to throw it out quicker'n a cat can lick its ass."

Had me by the short hair on a downhill pull and I knowed it, said, "Well, it all come down on me pretty quick." He didn't say nothing, I said, "I got what figures to be the murder weapon out in the car, I reckon you'll want that."

Said, like he didn't give a piddling shit either way, "Give it to Mrs. Winstead out front." Went to studying some papers on his desk.

━━━━━━━━━━

Wrote out a report that night, sent Harley over there with it the next morning, but the sheriff was right. Got a notice from his office bout a week later, said Mrs. Berotelli's case had been throwed out for lack of evidence.

Got to thinking about Mrs. Berotelli, that pearly white skin and them fruited plains, couple of days later sent Harley down there to check on her, instructed him to tell her if she needed help getting her life back in order I'd be pleased to come out there and give her solace.

Bout an hour later Harley come back, said he seen Mrs. Berotelli all right, said she didn't seem bitter or nothing bout what happened. She told him her and the boy was going to stay on, make what they could out of that rackety farm.

Maybe could a fertilized and raised a crop of cockleburr.

Harley said he told Mrs. Berotelli bout my christian offer to come and give her succor through them troublous times, she give him a note to bring back to me.

Note said, "Fuck you, Jack!"

Harley said, "Jack? Might be she's got you mixed up with somebody else."

I said, "Might be, Harley, but at the moment that ain't a theory I'm pushing."

After the Berotelli case the law business come nearly to a standstill. Late summer days, nothing moving, time slow and easy as sunsets over Butternut mountain.

Had now and then to go pick up Moose Thompson, stick him in that hotbox on the hill till he'd sweated the demons out of his sotted soul. One night got a call to go out to Duffy's tavern and quell a disturbance, but time I got out there it was over. Duffy said the combatants had done quelled each other, made up, and went home. Like Harley said, looked for awhile there like we'd done broke the crime wave in Cotterfield.

But I reckon like the good book says, They ain't no balm in Gilead and the spectre of tribulations is everwhere loose in the land.

Come on a Saturday, hot as the hinges of hell, me and Henry was sitting in the office having a fly swatting contest, little woman come in, one of them apple-faced granny types, borned to talk the dead up from the grave.

Said, "Marshal, my name's Emma Calhoun, most folks calls me Aunt Emma, ask anybody in Cotterfield they'll tell you bout Aunt Emma, I ain't one to make trouble, try to be a good neighbor, live and let live's my creed, I ain't a vengeful woman, anybody'll tell you that, don't think I ain't give long and solemn thought to what I'm doing."

I said, "Yes, mam, and what is it you're doing?"

She said, "I come to swear out a complaint on Mrs. Dinkins and them dogs."

I said, "And what might be the nature of your complaint?"

She said, "Impudence and disturbing the peace, them dogs barks night and day, don't never let up, I ain't had a good night's sleep since she moved in two weeks ago. I ask her more than once couldn't she calm them dogs down, didn't do a smidgen of good, went back over there this morning, she throwed a rotten apple at me, called me a name."

I said, "And what name was that?"

She said, "I'd liefer not say."

I said, "Well, they ain't no law against calling somebody a name."

She said, "She called me a old fart."

Heard Henry giggle, let that pass, said, "Also, they ain't no law against impudence. Was, my chief interrogator would be doing a life sentence. How many dogs we talking about?"

She said, "Lordy, I couldn't rightly say, she brought five or six with her, took to driving around on the county roads looking for strays, must have near a dozen now."

I said, "You ain't talked to Mr. Dinkins?"

She said, "I ain't sure they is no Mr. Dinkins, man come out there with her but I ain't seen him around the last week, I reckon them yapping dogs run him off."

I said, "I ain't saying you ain't got a good case, mam, onliest thing I ain't had no complaints from nobody else."

She said, "Course you ain't, don't nobody live out there but me and her, five miles out the old Black Hill road, another mile back in the woods. She first come I welcomed the company, gets lonely out there, only since she moved in I ain't had nothing but torment and miserations."

One of them pesky cases, wasn't going to get no better till it got worse. Said, "Well, mam, we'll just get in the car and drive out there, see can we resolve this here matter in a friendly and reasonable fashion."

She said, "Be a daresome thing I went back out there with you, I'd appreciate it you don't bring my name into it, that woman finds out it was me turned her in, ain't no telling what kind of meanness she'd do on me."

She give me directions how to get there and left, Henry said, "You want me to ride with you?"

I said, "I reckon you better, this here looks like one of them cases that's going to need some serious interrogation."

We come to the Black Hill cutoff a little after noon, drove a ways on till we seen the Garret Snuff sign nailed to a fence post, turned there and followed the wagon trail another mile back in the piney woods.

House sit back on a little knoll in a grove of trees, not much more than a shotgun shack, porch buckled at one end. Dogs everwhere, under the house, on the porch, under the pines up the hill, all shapes, sizes, and colors. We drove up they come from all directions, barking, yelping, howling. Country dogs don't need no good reason to set up a racket, it comes second nature to them. Sounded mostly like courtesy barking but you can't never tell, sit a minute thinking about it then honked a couple of times and waited. Minute later a woman come out of the house, stood on the porch shading her eyes against the sun, more girl than woman, maybe twenty years old, wearing baggy army britches and a man's shirt, hair down to her waist the color of laid by corn.

Waited a little, she didn't make no move, said to Henry, "Ask her does them dogs bite."

Henry stuck her head out the window, yelled, "How bout calling off them fucking dogs!"

Henry.

Woman come down the steps and across the yard, wading through them hounds, patting their heads as she come, got out there she give us a sweet smile, said, "Why them dogs ain't going to hurt nobody, they's God's creatures."

I got out, eased around there, said, "You Mrs. Dinkins?"

Talking slow, saying each word distinct, she said, "Yes, sir, I am. Reba Dell Dinkins, that's my name, praise the Lord."

Seen her shirt was unbuttoned bout halfway down, beheld inside the soft curve of a pearly globe, felt a twitch in my groin. Always the same, forbid fruit. A man ain't nothing but what he is.

Said, "I wonder, mam, could we just step inside and have a few words, them dogs is beginning to wear me down."

She said, "Course we can." Said to the dogs, "Y'all behave yourself."

Me and Henry followed her inside, room littered with toesacks and empty cans, unmade bed in one corner, panful of dirty dishes on the table. Seen in another corner a black and tan hound with a bloody bandage on his front paw. We come in he raised his head and give a little growl.

Mrs. Dinkins said, "That there's Moses, poor thing got his foot caught in a coon trap, looked for awhile like he wasn't going to make it but me and the Lord pulled him through, praise his holy name." Wasn't exactly clear whether it was Moses or the Lord got his holy name praised, she said, "Y'all want something to drink, they's some RC colars back there."

I said, "That'd be fine."

She just stood there, looking off in space, then more like talking to herself than us she said, "Judy Ray was mean to me, used to come in there, pinch me till I was black and blue, it was her told Mrs. Copeland I stole them eggs." Bout a minute passed, then it was like she come back from wherever she'd gone off to, she said, "Well, I'll get them colars."

Soon as she was gone Henry said, "Crazy as Aunt Lutie's goat, ain't she?"

I said, "Well now, I think you're a little hasty there, Miss Henry, little strange maybe but that ain't saying she's crazy."

She give me that sideways look, said, "I seen you ogling her out there, she's done hooked your ass ain't she?"

I said, "Ain't nobody hooked nobody's ass, whatever the hell that means."

She said, "Means you don't mend your ways you're going to one day drop dead with peckeritus."

I said, "Sister Henry, I wonder would you kindly do me a favor, just keep them foul thoughts to yourself."

Mrs. Dinkins come back with the pop, said, "They ain't no ice, I got a old refrigeratcr back there but they ain't no electricity to run it."

I ain't exactly crazy about hot RCs but took a swig anyway, didn't want to hurt nobody's feelings. Said, "Now, Mrs. Dinkins, they's certain duties a lawman's swore to carry out . . . ."

Bout then that far off look come in her eyes again, she said, "I never took them eggs, it was Judy Ray done it, I seen her with my own eyes . . . ."

I said, "Well, I don't know nothing about no eggs . . . ."

She said, "I told Mrs. Copeland but she wouldn't leave me be, they treated me bad up there . . . ."

I said, "Mrs. Dinkins." She just stood there, looking down at the floor. I laid my hand on her shoulder, said, "Mrs. Dinkins." Counted ten.

Finally she looked up, smiled, said, "Don't pay me no mind, I runs on sometimes."

Felt sorry for her but done what I come to do, said, "Mrs. Dinkins, they's been a complaint filed against you and them dogs."

She said, "Poor Mrs. Calhoun, God bless her sweet soul..."

I said, "She says them dogs bark day and night, says she can't get no sleep . . . ."

She said, "It's natural dogs to bark, ain't it?"

I said, "Mrs. Calhoun says she come over to talk about it, you called her names, throwed a apple at her . . . ."

She said, "Why I never throwed no apple at her, I might a kind of tossed it towards her, just playful, you know how old folks gets things mixed up."

I said, "Well, I reckon that's your word against hers, but we still got a problem bout them dogs barking."

She stood a little thinking about it, said, "What is it you aim to do?"

I said, "I ain't got no choice, you and Mrs. Calhoun can't settle this peaceable, I'll have to take you and them dogs to court."

She didn't say nothing for a little, then turned and walked over and stood looking out the window, finally without turning around she said, "I'll pray about it. I'll ask God to show me the way. God is my strength and redeemer. Praise his holy name." After a little she turned, said, "Don't worry no more about it, it'll be took care of."

Maybe that was a answer, maybe it wasn't. Remember now a strange feeling come over me, seemed like they was something ought to be said but I couldn't think what it was, finally I said, "Well, you look after yourself."

Me and Henry went and got in the car, them dogs still barking as we drove off down the hill. Wasn't nothing said for a mile or so, finally Henry said, "Spooky, ain't it?"

I said, "I reckon that's the word for it."

Rode a little on, she said, "What you figure that loony woman's going to do?"

I said, "Knowed that, Sister Henry, might be I'd know what to do my ownself."

Got back to town I let Henry off at the office, spent the rest of the day driving around, going nowhere, doing nothing, restless as a caged coyote. Truth was I couldn't got that dog woman off my mind. Wasn't none of Henry's peckeritus afflicting me, something else, hard to say just what, like I knowed they was something ought to be done but couldn't figure out what it was. Could in my mind hear that woman saying, "Don't worry no more about it, it'll be took care of."

Slept fitful that night, bedeviled by diresome dreams, up at first light, went and sit on the back porch watching the sun rise slow through the mulberry tree, listening to sweet birdsongs in the thicket along the fence. Wasn't no peace in it. Times it takes more than birdsongs to ease a troubled heart.

Little later Henry come out there, stood a minute looking at me, said, "You want some breakfast?"

I said, "No."

She sit down, didn't say nothing for a little, said, "You going back out there?"

I said, "Yes, mam, I reckon I better."

She said, "You want me to go along?"

I said, "No, somebody needs to mind the office."

She said, "You're worried, ain't you?"

I said, "Ain't exactly worried, little anxious maybe."

She said, "Likely you ain't going to find nothing out there but them yapping dogs and that befuzzled woman."

I said, "Likely."

Sit a little longer, she said, "I better go fix Harley some breakfast, he ain't but barely tolerable till he's eat."

She was gone I sit another little while, trying I reckon to talk myself out of what I knowed had to be done, finally give her up, got in the batmobile and set out for the piney woods.

Got to Black Hill cutoff a little after eight, little ways on come to Mrs. Calhoun's house, sit across the road at the bottom of the hill, stopped there but couldn't raise nobody, house locked, got back in the car and drove ahead on. Seen the devastation as I come over the rise, as pitiful a sight as ever I behelt, house sitting peaceful up there on the knoll, front yard littered with the bodies of them poor dead dogs. Drove on up, seen when I got out they'd been poisoned, bug-eyed, tongues hanging out, teeth bared. Four or five crawled under the front porch, others left belly tracks in the dust trying to get there. Strange how a poisoned dog will strive to crawl under cover before he dies.

Stood there amidst that carnage, sick in my belly, crazy thought crossed my mind, was they any law against poisoning your own dogs?

Went across to the house and up on the porch, seen her through the screen door, sitting there at the table shelling peas and humming a little tune.

I come in she looked up, a kind of smile on her face, said, "I been thinking bout you, wondering would you come back." Stood up, said, "You want something to drink."

I said, "No, mam, I don't, what I want's to know who killed them poor misbegotten dogs out there."

She just stood there a good little while, looking down at the floor, finally said, "Them dogs was mean to me."

Slipping looked like into another one of them spells, I said, "You didn't say nothing bout no mean dogs I was out here yesterday."

Never even heard me, mind off somewheres else, said, "Them dogs was sent by the devil." I waited her out, then heard her say, "Same as Luther."

Thought, Lordamighty, hoping I'd mistook what she said, tried a shot off the wall, said, "Luther another one of them dogs?"

She said, "My man."

Count twenty, took a deep breath, remembered Mrs. Calhoun said a man come with her when she moved in, said, "Where's Luther at now?"

She said, "Out yonder in the woods." Quiet a minute, said, "He was meaning to hurt me."

Can't say now what I felt then. Numb I reckon. Like I'd done stumbled into a bad dream, said, "I reckon you better show me where Luther's at."

Didn't say nothing atall, just turned and went out the back way. I followed her through the woods, maybe quarter of a mile till we come to a long spiney ridge, thought it must a took that snit of a woman half a day to drag a body all that way through them piney hills.

Smelt Luther fore I seen him. Little ways on we come to a shallow ravine, woman stopped and pointed, seen down there Luther's mortal remains, what they was left to see. Been mutilated by varmits, them dogs maybe, face half eat away, arms and legs mangled. Stood a minute, soul weary and sick at heart, breathing through my mouth against the stench, onliest sounds was the swarming flies and the pines rustling in the breeze. I seen dead men before but nothing like that, death and devastation in them quiet peaceful woods, didn't make no sense atall.

I looked at the woman, a pitiful sight standing there with her head down, hair hanging across her face. Said, "I'm going to have to take you to town."

She give me a frighted look, said, "You ain't fixing to hurt me are you?"

I said, "No, mam, ain't nobody going to hurt you."

Went back to the house, let her get some clothes, went and put her in the car and set out for the county seat. Woman never said nothing, just sit slumped against the door, empty look on her face, I reckon off somewhere in a world I didn't know nothing about.

Riding along there I got to thinking, which was where it all started. Got to thinking about all them years I spent up at Pordell, them guards savaging my ass I so much as give them a slant look, laying on that bunk at night too tired to sleep, yearning for the sight of quail flushed up from a dried beanfield or the sweet sound of meadowlarks singing at sunup. All them wasted years biding my time against the day I'd walk out of there a free man. Come to me then for the first time, damn near blowed me away. Thought, Godamighty, boy, all them years you spent locked up in that peafarm prison and here you are bout to send that poor bedeviled woman to the same place, there or up to the nuthouse at Delhurst which is maybe worse. Seen I was into something needed thinking through, tried telling myself somebody had to keep the law and order but knowed I was just pissing in the wind. Had come to a mighty crossroads.

Little ways on come to a creek ford, pulled off to one side and stopped, said to the woman, "I'll be back directly, don't get out of the car, I'm watching you."

She said, "I ain't going nowhere."

Got out and walked aways down the creek, sit down on a flat rock and done some more thinking. Where I come out was, maybe it was all wrote down somewheres a thousand years ago how it was going to be, how it was going to be I'd go to that dance over in Milo and see Ada standing there by the window looking somehow lonely, how it was going to be I would come home early from squirrel hunting and catch Larry Lee ravishing my wayward woman, all long ago wrote down somewheres, how I'd serve time up at Pordell and how after I got out I'd be called to preach the gospel, how me and Harley would pick up where we left off and I'd take up with and come to care for a foul-mouthed freckle-faced pissant of a girl that I never wanted or needed, how I'd end up in the law business, sitting on a flat rock trying to figure out what the hell I was going to do with a poor demented woman that didn't have nowhere to turn and nothing to hope for. Maybe should a give some thought to Luther but the way I figured it they wasn't no hellova lot I could do for him.

I ain't saying what I done was right, ain't saying it was wrong, what I done I done and that's the word with the bark on it. Mostly a man's got to live with hisself, I've give it quite a lot of thought and what I come to is this, give the same situation I can't think of nothing I'd do different.

Went back up there, woman had done put despair behind her. Said, "I been watching them two squirrels playing in that oak tree, they's the cutest things."

I said, "Mam, you got any people?"

She said, "People?"

I said, "Family."

She said, "Got a sister lives in Oklahoma."

I said, "Where bouts in Oklahoma?"

She said, "Her and Herman lives on a farm little ways out of Stillwater."

I said, "You went there, you reckon they'd take you in?"

She said, "I reckon so, I ain't seen Della Mae in ten years. Me and her always got along good."

So that was it, knowed what I had to do, never had no doubts or looked back. Got in the car and drove on to the cutoff, took a left there, hanged highway 4 down below Briley's store and set out for Malcolmville."

Rode a little ways, woman said, "You taking me to jail?"

I said, "No, mam, I ain't, I'm taking you to the bus station over at Malcolmville."

That perked her up, said, "I ain't rode a bus since I can't remember when, where we going?"

Said, "I ain't going nowheres, you're going to Oklahoma, see can you find aid and comfort with your sister Della Mae."

She said, "They ain't going to lock me up?"

I said, "I reckon they can't lock you up they don't know where you're at. Thing you got to remember is to not say nothing to nobody bout what happened back at Mud Creek."

She sit a little looking out the window, said, "Luther was fixing to hurt me."

Thought crossed my mind, ain't too late to take her in. Said, "Damn it, woman, I don't know nothing bout no misunderstanding you and Luther had, onliest thing I do know is Luther's been dispatched and it was you that done it. What you got to do is put that out of your mind, just tell yourself it never happened, don't talk to nobody when you get on that bus, and don't say nothing bout Luther to Herman and Della Mae, cause if it's ever found out they're going to put you and me where the birds don't sing and the creek don't rise."

She didn't say nothing, just sit there looking out the window, my patience running thin, I said, "You listening!"

She said, "I ain't deaf."

Got to Malcolmville round eleven o'clock, railroad runs through the center of town, rightaway littered and growed up in weeds. Place you'd maybe stop for a cup of coffee on your way somewheres else.

Drove a little ways down main street, stopped and queried a weazily looking kid, said the bus station was in the back of Hester's cafe down at the lower end of town.

Got down there, sit a little out front sizing up the scene, nobody coming or going, said to the woman, "I don't reckon you got no money?"

Reckoned right, hadn't over-expected on that, didn't figure I'd got myself mixed up with no hairess. Told her to stay in the car, went over to a window and done a little reconnoitering, sure as hell didn't want to encounter no law officer. Seen in there standing at the cash register counting change a moon-faced woman with orange hair, old fart wearing one of them goat roper hats hunkered over the counter nursing a cup of coffee, ticket cage in back, somebody behind that. Went and got the woman, took her inside and sit her down at a booth in the back corner.

Hester said, "Y'all want to see a menu?"

Said to the woman, "You hungry?"

She said, "I ain't eat nothing since yesterday, anything's all right."

Ordered her a cheeseburger and a RC cola, went back to the ticket cage, slack-jawed boy standing there rifling through some tickets, greasy hair hanging down to his shoulders. I tapped on the counter, he didn't look up or say nothing, one of them boys that can't hardly make a living working for what he's worth.

I said, "What time you got a bus for Stillwater, Oklahoma?"

Kept counting them tickets, mouth hanging open, another one of them brilliant public servants. Finally laid the tickets down, said "Is they something I can do for you?"

Said, "Well, I ain't too fucking sure of that, I need a one way ticket to Stillwater, Oklahoma, reckon you can bring that off?"

He give me a sullen look, seen he wanted to say something but thought better of it, took up a dog-eared ticket book and started writing. Took him another five minutes to figure out the price, finally said, "That'll be thirty-four fifty, bus'll be here in forty-five minutes, change to Greyhound in Lehigh, half hour lay over, puts you in Stillwater eight fifteen tonight."

Paid him and went back to the booth, woman sitting there looking lorn, hadn't eat more than a bite or two of the cheeseburger. Told her bout the bus, how she'd have to change at Lehigh, said again, "Don't talk to nobody bout what happened back at mud creek, fact don't talk to nobody bout nothing."

Give her the ticket, seen in her eyes the fear and loneliness, she said, "You ain't going to wait till the bus comes?"

Touched my heart but I'd done thought about that. Way I seen it she had to go it alone sooner or later, I sure as hell couldn't escort her all the way to Oklahoma. Said, "No, mam, I ain't, they's things I got to do back in Cotterfield."

Put twenty dollars on the table, bout what I had, she just left it lay there, sit with her head down, I said, "You going to be all right?"

She didn't look up, said, "I reckon."

I didn't know what else to say, wasn't nothing else I could do, give her a pat on the shoulder and walked away.

Many's the time I wondered what happened to that desolated woman, locked up somewheres I reckon, borned to travail and tribulations. Think I knowed the day I left her that they wasn't nobody could save her from pain and suffering. I give it quite a lot of thought and where I come out is, maybe what I done I done for my ownself.

Long ways from Malcolmville to Cotterfield, longer you take a wrong turn, which is what I done. Come to mind seemed like since they let me out of Pordell I'd got to be some kind of a expert on wrong turns.

Found myself lost down in Saline river bottom, beset by one of them sudden thunderstorms, skies black as Coaly's ear, gale winds lashing the trees along the river, visibility somewheres around two feet, slithering along there bout ten miles a hour.

Got to thinking about things, where I'd been and where I was going, all them dead dogs, that woman sitting there staring at that uneat Cheeseburger, crying babies and Jesus on the cross. Give myself a hard talking to, said, shit, boy, they ain't no kind of storm that lasts forever, any poor bastard can feel sorry for hisself, like Aunt Heather always said, if it can't kill you it ain't nothing to worry about.

Home truth. Run out of the storm just this side of Thaxton, time I got to Mumford clear skies and sweet sunshine, gassed up and procured a six pack of Lone Star, flagged her for Cotterfield.

Drove up to the office round sundown, found Henry and Harley inside, Harley sitting asleep in a leaned back chair, Henry playing herself a game of checkers. She looked up, said, "Where the hell you been, me and Harley bout worried ourselves sick." I said, "Yeah, I can see things is pretty tense round here."

She said, "You left this morning you was on your way to check on that looney woman."

Said, "Well, that's what I done."

Went and sit down at the desk, her watching me, truth was I wasn't in no frame of mind to discuss that misbegotten day.

Henry said, "Well?"

I said, "Well, what?"

She said, "Claude Dee, you're bout pushing me to my limits, what'd you find out there?"

I said, "Found Luther, dispatched."

She said, "Who's Luther?"

Said, "Mrs. Dinkins' husband, I reckon."

She said, "Godamighty, she killed her husband?"

Said, "That's what she said."

She said, "It took you all day to take her in to the county seat?"

Said, "I didn't take her to no county seat, taken her over to Malcolmville and put her on a bus to Oklahoma, she's got people there."

Harley bestirred hisself, said, "You telling me you turned her loose?" Didn't see no reason to say it again, he said, "How come you done that?"

Said, "I ain't yet figured that out, Harley, soon as I do I'll let you know."

He said, "Shit, man, that makes you a accessory after the fact of the crime, what you call your prima facie."

Prima facie.

I said, "Harley, I don't need no half-assed deputy telling me the law."

Henry come up so fast she knocked over the checker-board, said, "Hell's fire, we ain't getting nowheres talking bout it, what we got to do is go into hiding."

I said, "Try to get ahold of yourself, Sister Henry, it ain't a foregone conclusion they're going to find that woman or what she done. Second place, I tried hiding out once after I shot and killed Larry Lee Ludlow. Went and stayed two days down in the river bottom, chiggers and mosquitoes damn near eat me alive, knowed anyhow they'd find me sooner or later no matter where I went, so I come out. Truth is, hiding ain't something I'm good at." Said to Harley, "Go down to the tool shed at the park, get three shovels and a couple of lanterns, we'll wait for you here."

Henry said, "Where we going?"

I said, "Right now we're going bury a dead man and some dead dogs, tomorrow we're going home."

Got out to the woman's place a little after eight o'clock, cut the car lights coming up the rise, parked in a grove of trees a little ways back off the road and got out. Seen them bloated dogs laying there twisted and still in the pale moonlight, already fermenting and beginning to smell.

Lit the lanterns and we went back up in the pines to where Luther laid a mouldering. Stood a minute looking at him. Henry said, "I'm fixing to puke."

I said, "Well, puke and get it over with, we got work to do." Worked maybe three hours digging that grave, long enough to hold Luther and all them dogs, deep enough so's varmits wouldn't come and scratch them up. Mosquitoes come down on us in swarms, digging and a slapping, slapping and a digging, hot as a blast furnace.

Finally got her finished, twelve foot long, maybe eight deep. Stood back and took a blow, sweating like we'd been fighting brush fires. Luther wasn't in no shape to be laid down gentle, so we shoveled him in, seen him hit crumpled, his head twisted to one side.

Wasn't nothing said for a minute, Harley said, "Gives you a funny feeling, don't it. You want me to jump down there and straighten him out?"

I said, "No, it ain't going to make no difference to Luther."

Went back down to the house and started bringing up them dogs, me and Harley dragging them by their hind legs, three or four at a time, Henry lighting the way with the lanterns, one of them solemn death marches, onliest sounds Harley grunting, now and then off in the woods the squawk of a night bird.

Getting on towards midnight when I put Harley and Henry to shoveling dirt back in the grave, went down to the house after the last carcass. That's when I seen it, something or somebody down by the road watching. Nothing I could clear make out, wasn't no more than a shadow, kind of hunkered down behind the buckleweed that growed along the cutbank, maybe fifty yards away. Stood there a minute looking down that way, holding the lantern over my head, my heart thumping like a sump pump. Truth was, I didn't have no idea what to do. Thought if they was somebody down there and I could run him down, what the hell was I gong to do after I caught him.

Started walking slow towards the road, bout halfway there seen a movement, or thought I did, shadows plays tricks on a moonlight night. Waited a little listening, then went ahead on, wanting I reckon whoever it was to be gone fore I come. Wanting I reckon to make myself believe they wasn't nobody there in the first place.

Nobody there, I wasn't looking for there to be, one part of my mind thinking I seen what I seen, other part thinking I'd done slipped a gear.

Got the dog and went back up in the pines, got up there seen Henry shoveling dirt, Harley sitting off to one side with his head between his knees.

Throwed the dog in the hole, said, "What's wrong with Harley?"

Henry said, "Having one of them heat strokes, I reckon. I ain't ask, he went and sit down soon as you was gone."

Went over there, said, "You all right?"

He said, "Heart attack feels like."

Said, "Well, them light ones don't amount to nothing. You ain't dead, chances are it ain't too severe."

He give me a mournful look, said, "You don't never feel sorry for nobody, do you?"

I said, "Feel sorry for damn near everbody, Harley. Rejoice with them that do rejoice, weep with them that is afflicted. That there's your Deuteronomy."

He said, "Deuteronomy's ass, that there's something you just made up."

Seen he was pretty touchy so let that pass.

Didn't say nothing bout what I seen down at the house. Little after midnight we got the grave covered, strewed it over with pine needles, stood there awhile in silent benefaction, air heavy with the stench of putrification.

Harley said, "You're a preacher, you ain't going to say no words of comfort?"

Said, "Reckon I can, Harley." Couldn't think of no scripture that said nothing bout dead dogs. Said, "Lord, as you can see these dogs and Luther is on their way. Dogs didn't do nothing to get killed for, can't speak for Luther. Anyways, we hope you'll do what you can for them when they arrive. Amen."

Still didn't nobody move, stood about a minute with our heads bowed, finally Henry said, "This here's been the worst fucking night of my life."

PART THREE

PORDELL REVISITED

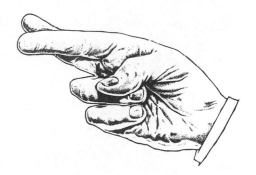

Really, if the lower orders don't set us a good example, what on earth is the use of them?

Oscar Wilde

Now therefore keep thy sorry to thyself and bear with good courage that which hath befallen thee.

The Aprocrypha (Esdras)

The gospel according to remembering the good times.

Claude Dee Moran Junior

Chapter Ten

Something one of them writers said in that study course I taken up at Pordell, said, home is a place you ain't got to deserve. Deserve. Set your mind on it, that there's a interesting word. Hear people say, well, he got what he deserved, or, well, he didn't deserve what he got. Don't nobody hardly ever say, well, he got what he got, which is about the onliest thing you need to know cause that's where the hammer comes down.

I ain't saying what I deserved or didn't deserve for packing that addled woman off to her sister in Oklahoma. What I do know is that's what started me thinking bout where I'd been, where I was at, and where I was going. And where I come out was I felt a deep yearning to go

back and start at the beginning, back to that persimmon
sprout farm where I dreamed a dream with Ada and heard
the crickets sing.

I've give it quite a lot of thought and here's where I
come out, ain't nothing more important than where you're
at and how you spend your days, cause in the end a man
creates his ownself. Take a fifteen-year-old boy, he gets it
in his mind he wants to be a big city lawyer so he goes
off to New York or somewheres, studies the law, don't think
about nothing much else, now when he's growed up he's
going to think and talk and act like a big city lawyer.
Take that same boy, say he gets it in his mind he wants
to go to some mountaintop in Montana and herd sheep,
he's growed up to be a man is he going to think and talk
and act like a big city lawyer? Course he ain't, going to
think, talk, and act like a mountain sheepherder. Boy's
done changed hisself into a different person cause he done
one thing and not the other. That there's pretty interesting
you think about it. Says a man can pretty much decide
in his own mind what it is he wants to be.

I ain't making judgments, lawyer, sheepherder, revival
preacher, town marshal, all comes down to what you want.
For me after that sorrowful night in the piney woods it
come down to that gulley-wash farm where I started. Come
down to putting seed in the ground, watching thunderstorms make up over Butternut mountain, listening
to the cicadas singing in the fields as dusk settles in.
Come down to biding my time till the dream come true.

Way things turned out they wasn't much time to bide.
Seems a long time ago I dreamt myself a hill farmer but
ain't nothing that's happened has changed that, cause the
onliest thing that's real's the dream.

―――――――――

Morning after the night we buried Luther and them
dogs we packed the car and drove into town, I turned the

keys to the squad car over to Colonel Suggs, tendered him our resignations, told him the truth, said we'd been called by the Lord to till the soil and harvest the fruits thereof.

I got to Howtown bout the middle of the afternoon, first thing on my mind was Aunt Heather, drove over there and parked under the mulberry tree, seen her sitting on the porch in that highback rocker, head leaned a little to one side, done dozed off.

We got out and went up there, seemed like she'd shrunk since last I seen her, all skin and bones, a once strong woman growed old and frail with time, ain't nothing sadder than that. Thought come to me. Thought, all them years she taken care of me, whatever I needed, whenever I needed it, comes now my time to take care of her.

I said, "Aunt Heather?" She stirred but didn't wake.

Henry said, "Bless her heart."

I put my hand on her shoulder, give her a little shake, said, "It's me, Aunt Heather, Claude Dee Junior."

She opened her eyes, sit a minute trying to get her bearings, leaned a little forward, said, "Claude Dee Junior?"

I said, "Yes, mam, come to see how you're getting along."

She said, "Getting along fine, same as always, thought you was working as a marshal over at Cotterfield."

Said, "Not no more I ain't, learnt the hard way I ain't cut out to be a lawman."

She said, "Ask me, they's a good chance you ain't cut out for nothing, there's them that ain't."

I said, "Not me, figure I'm cut out to be a free man, don't want to mess with nobody, don't want nobody messing with me."

She said, "Ain't going to be free long as you're running helter skelter, one place and another, where you going next?"

Said, "Ain't going nowheres, come home this time to stay, Lord's done called us to till the fields, going to clean up that farm, hold on through the winter, plant a crop next spring. Lord said, Go forth and live by the sweat of your brow, put seed in the ground and harvest the fruits thereof."

She said, "Well, looks like the Lord's done gone to backing long shots."

I said, "Ain't backing no long shot this time, we aim to work day and night, that's what it takes, make something out there where they ain't nothing now." Said, "Something else we aim to do's take you out there with us, put you in charge of sundowns and peach cobblers."

She said, "Ain't nobody taking me nowheres, let alone out to some claybank farm, getting old maybe but I ain't yet lost my mind."

I said, "Aunt Heather, I ain't running off no more, you taken care of me all them years, man and boy, comes time now I take care of you."

She said, "Don't need no taking care of, take care of my ownself, time comes I can't I'll turn myself in down at the Rest Home." Pushed herself up, made it on the second try, held on to the chair till she stopped wobbling, said, "I reckon you're all hungry."

One thing I knowed, my Aunt Heather wasn't going in no nursing home, I said, "Aunt Heather . . . ." But she'd done gone in the house.

Harley said, "She's proud, ain't she?"

I said, "Proud or stubborn, whichever way you look at it."

I went and offered to help in the kitchen but she give me leave to stay out of her way, went back to the living room seen Harley and Henry standing over by the table looking at that wartime picture of Uncle Edgar.

I come in, Henry said, "Who's this weazily looking guy?"

Just come out, said, "That there's my Uncle Edgar, give his life for his country in World War I, decorated four or five times for bravery, what you call your boni fide hero."

She said, "Don't look like no hero to me."

I said, "Well now, why don't you tell me what a hero's supposed to look like."

She said, "I don't know, strong I reckon. Uncle Edgar ain't got no chin, looks like one of them corn bin rats."

I said, "He can't help it he ain't got no chin . . . ."

She said, "Them beady little eyes . . . ."

They's limits, said, "Damn it, Henry. . . ."

She said, "How'd he get killed?"

Done gone that far, said, "Storming one of them German pill boxes, single-handed, just him against eight Germans, wiped them scutters out with hand grenades, wading through a hail of machine gun fire, last grenade blowed up in his hand, they never found nothing but his belt buckle."

She give me a sly look, said, "Ask me, that there's just something you made up."

Said, "I ain't heard nobody ask you."

Harley said, "I thought he was killed in a truck wreck."

I said, "Ain't nobody ask you either."

Henry said, "Aunt Heather got any of them medals he won?"

I said, "I done terminated this discussion, Sister Henry, why don't you go out to the kitchen, see is they something you can help Aunt Heather with."

Got over to the door she said, "I never said he wasn't no hero, said he didn't look like no hero." Kept on a walking.

Harley standing there, a silly grin on his face, said, "She's a kick in the ass, ain't she?"

Said, "You shore got a way with words, Harley."

Little while later Aunt Heather called us to come eat, done fixed my favorite meal, cow peas, fried okra, sweet

tators, collard greens, johnny bread and salt pork, first
home cooked meal we'd sit down to since we left town,
Harley said it come to eating he took after his whole
family, eat lots like his pa, fast like his ma, took big bites
like old Shep.

We was done I offered to help wash up the dishes but
Aunt Heather wouldn't have none of that, said washing
dishes was woman's work. Said I wished the hell she'd a
knowed that I was growing up a boy.

She walked out to the car with us, I give her a kiss,
said, "I ain't give up on you yet, soon as we get settled
want you to move out to the farm, give you the big bedroom,
won't have to do nothing but sit on the porch and rock."

Something I had cause to remember later, she said,
"Chances are you'd be gone fore I got there."

We got in the car and drove off, her still standing there
under the mulberry tree, we turned the corner she give
a little wave, missing us already, though she wouldn't a
said so you held a loaded gun to her head.

Stopped at the mill commissary and procured a few
supplies, picked up a cooler, bag of ice, and a case of beer
at the Red Rooster, set out for the farm.

Got there just as the sun was going down, house from
the rise looked smaller than I remembered it, half in
shadows, fields already brown from summer heat sloping
down to the creek, sky above Butternut streaked with red
and gold. Right then felt something for the land I hadn't
never felt before, not even when me and Ada moved out
there seemed like a hundred years ago, thought, everbody's got a place where they belong, even if they don't
know where it's at, maybe this here's mine.

Parked in the back yard, got the car unloaded, then sit
on the porch drinking beer and watching night coming
on. Wasn't no sound but the far off barking of a dog, sit
awhile without nobody saying nothing, Harley said, "You
serious bout us farming this place?"

Said, "I ain't never been more serious bout nothing in my life."

He said, "Take some doing, this here's piss poor land."

Said, "They ain't no land so poor it won't grow something."

He said, "What we supposed to use for money, we're damn near broke, ain't got so much as a rusty turning plow or a choleric mule."

Done thought about that, said, "Bank opens in the morning I'll be first in line, deed to this farm in my pocket, ought to let us have enough against it to get what we need and see us through the winter."

Harley finished his beer and got up, said, "Well, I'm bout peckered out, seems like I ain't never ready for morning." Stood there, seen he had something else he wanted to say, said, "I ain't scared of hard work."

I said, "I know you ain't, Harley, this here's yours and Henry's farm same as mine, ours to make something out of or fail at, be enough hard work to go round."

He was gone I sit looking at Henry, hunkered down on the bottom step staring off at the night, said, "You ain't had much to say, Sister Henry, you all right?"

After a little she said, "We never should a left this farm."

Said, "Don't do no good to look back, we're here now."

Quiet again, finally she said, "I can't stop thinking bout that woman, she tells them what happened they're going to come looking for you, don't you never think of that?"

I said, "Now and then I reckon, try not to, thinking bout it ain't going to change nothing. Here on in we go it one day at a time."

Chapter Eleven

First thing next morning went to the bank in Howtown
and done some serious negotiating with old man Brewster,
told him I needed to borrow five thousand dollars against
the farm, knowed he wouldn't spring for that. He said the
land out there wouldn't grow a good stand of buckleweed,
said anyways fall loans was risky, to come back and talk
to him in the spring. Didn't surprise me none, bankers is
born to prey on dirt farmers and widow women, reminded
him I bought the farm with a loan from his bank, never
missed a payment, got off on Aunt Heather, said she was
afflicted with old age and other decrepicies and needed
looking after, quoted a few scriptures that bore directly
on my case, come away with twenty-five hundred, bout
twice what I figured to get.

Put the money in our acccunt, went over to see Gussie, another one of life's horses' asses, dickered with him for half a hour, left him the batmobile and four hundred dollars, drove out a flatbed Ford truck with one fender missing, needed new plugs and rings but nothing else that couldn't wait.

Stopped at Tooter's garage and bought what parts I needed, borrowed some tools, then drove out to Farm Equipment Rentals on Camel Hill, procured a bushhog, twenty dollars a week, loaded it on the flatbed and set out for home.

Got out there found Harley and Henry down at the barn lot, Harley cutting weeds along the fencerow, flailing away like he was fighting off a swarm of riled up hornets, Henry on top of the barn nailing down a strip of sprung sheet iron. Thought, Lordamighty, them two's done caught the spirit of our endeavors can't nothing stop us.

Parked out back, they come on up there, Harley circled the flatbed, give the tires a kick, said, "Where'd you get this here war relic?

Said, "Bought her from Gussie, she's ours free and clear, got us a truck, a rented bushhog, money in the bank."

He stood there looking where the fender was missing, stuck his head through the window, backed off and shook his head, said, "Give more than a couple of rat turds for it, you give too much."

I said, "Runs better than she looks, needs new plugs and rings, little fine tuning, nothing I can't do myself." Seen he wasn't convinced, said, "We sure as hell couldn't a done no farming out of that batmobile."

He said, "Yeah, well . . . ." Meant you done fucked up, ain't nothing I can do about it now.

Henry said, "How we going to get that bushhog down from there?"

I said, "Ain't no hurry bout that, might be we ought to take a break, treat ourselves to a cold Lone Star."

Harley said, "Shit, man, we stop to drink a beer evertime somebody works up a little thirst we ain't never going to get this farm cleaned up."

Looked at Henry, she give a little shrug, I said, "Harley, I ain't yet figured out what it's going to be, but first thing in the morning I'm putting you in charge of something."

Early next morning we set in on the field west of the house, fifteen acres growed up in cockleburr and shank briar, can still in my mind see Henry bouncing round on that bucking bushhog, times hid from sight by swirling dust, me and Harley following behind hand raking for burning what the bushhog didn't mulch.

Times laying awake at night I think about them first days back on the farm, everthing going our way, what we couldn't do for our ownselves somebody done for us. Looked for awhile there like we'd done got her turned around.

Took us two days to finish bushhogging that field, next morning Harley taken the bushhog back to town, me and Henry was up there burning brush, bout the middle of the morning seen a pickup truck turn off the road, drive slow up the wagon trail. Fellar got out, lean lank jake with a gimpy leg, come walking up there where we was, said, "Hot work, ain't it?"

First thing come in my mind was what happened over at Cotterfield and had he come to take me away. Didn't look like no lawman, driving a pickup truck, wearing overhauls and a straw hat, didn't have no badge showing, still he wasn't nobody I'd ever saw before.

I said, "Something that's got to be done."

He stuck out his hand, said, "Name's George Ferguson, live a couple of miles down the road."

We shook, I give him my name, said, "This here's Miss Henry Hesterman."

Henry stood there glaring, didn't make no move to shake hands.

Mr. Ferguson said, "You folks put in long hours, come by here early yesterday morning, you was up here bush-hogging this field, come back a little fore dark, you was still at it."

Said, "Well, we only just moved out here, farm's laid fallow four years, they's a lot of cleaning up to do fore it's ready for planting."

He said, "Ain't been here but a couple of years myself, moved down from Kansas." Give me a steady look, said, "I heered about you, people talk."

Said, "Yeah, well I ain't got nothing to hide."

He said, "Understand it don't make no difference to me what a man's done, I take him where he's at and go ahead on." Didn't say nothing to that, he said, "You aiming to seed this field?"

Said, "We ain't thought that far ahead, ain't got much equipment, right now no money to buy none, just doing what has to be done, trying to stay one day ahead of yesterday."

He didn't say nothing for a minute, then said, "I got equipment, you're welcome to use whatever you need, I ain't using it myself, disc up this field might be it'll grow winter wheat."

Said, "Well, we're obliged to you."

He said, "Pleasures me to see young folks ain't afraid of hard work, ain't many of them left, come get whatever you need, I ain't there tell my woman, my farm's first one on the right after you cross Pedigo creek bridge."

Couldn't think of nothing else to say, said again, "We're obliged to you."

He walked off down the hill, watched till he got in his truck and drove off, said, "I reckon they's somebody looking out for us, Miss Henry."

She said, "And I was done ready for the worst. You know what I thought I first seen him walking up that rise?"

Said, "Yeah, same thing crossed my mind. Running scared, I reckon, you start looking for trouble where they ain't none."

━━━━━━━━━━

Them was good times, while they lasted. Little over three weeks we worked that farm, planted turnips where the old garden used to be, sowed the rest of the field in winter wheat, disced and planted white clover in the lower pasture, figured maybe we'd later run a few sheep, mended the fence along the creek, put a new roof on the barn and finished painting the house. Working dawn till dusk, twelve, fourteen hours a day, nobody letting up long as they was light to work by, place beginning to look like the county demonstration farm. End of the day, drag our-selves down to the creek, wash off the sweat and dust, go back up to the house and sit awhile on the porch, listening to them lonely hounds wailing off in the night, proud of what we done but too wore out to talk about it.

On the seventh day we rested, remembered the Sabbath and kept it holy, lay in bed till we got ready to get up, Henry'd maybe putter around in them wild flowers, me and Harley'd sit out there under the mulberry tree, drink a few beers, do a little casual whittling, he'd sometimes break out in one of them solos, otherwise quiet and peaceful.

Middle of the afternoon I'd drive to town, bring Aunt Heather back out there, sit and visit awhile, later she'd fix up one of them field hand suppers, then while Henry and Harley was cleaning up the kitchen me and her would walk down to the creek, along the bank aways to the willow grove, sit there as the sun went down talking bout one thing and another. Like old people, will she'd get off on how things used to be back when I was a boy, I reckon looking for something back there to hold on to, talking mostly bout things I'd heard before but it give her pleasure to remember, give me pleasure to listen.

Things I remember my ownself, but nothing don't last forever.

Wouldn't be the truth I said them first days back on the farm I never thought about what was hanging over me. Times at night, too tired to sleep, I'd go over it in my mind step by step, from the time I seen them dead dogs till I walked out of that cafe in Malcolmville, that sorrowful woman sitting slumped in a corner booth staring at a half eat cheeseburger. Couldn't help thinking bout it but it wasn't nothing I brooded over, cause I knowed it was already worked out, how it was going to be, who was going to dance and who was going to pay the fiddler. Couldn't do nothing bout that, so the onliest thing that mattered was what you done when it come your turn to pay up.

Human nature to hope, after awhile, another day come and went without nothing happening, got to thinking maybe wasn't nothing going to happen. Maybe that woman wasn't never going to be found out, maybe I was home free.

Hope don't cost nothing. Truth was I never believed that. Truth was I knowed deep in my heart that soon or late they'd be there.

━━━━━━━━━

They come on a rainy Monday morning just at daybreak, county sheriff and two of his deputies. I was done up and dressed, sitting on the side of the bed smoking a cigarette, heard the car coming over the rise, stop at the end of the wagon lane. Went to the window and watched, seen them get out, stand there still as gravestones looking towards the house. Didn't feel nothing, seemed like something I'd been waiting for all my life.

Went out the front door, stood there a minute amid Henry's wild flowers, felt the rain on my face.

They didn't move, just stood there watching me, sheriff a big man with a pot belly, both deputies holding shotguns.

Walked slow up the rise, got up there said, "They something I can help you with?"

Sheriff said, "Claude Dee Moran?"

I said, "Yes, sir. Junior."

He said, "I reckon you know why we're here?"

I said, "I can't say as I do."

He said, "You're under arrest." Said to one of the deputies, "Read him his rights."

Deputy took a piece of paper out of his shirt pocket, read me my rights, sheriff said, "You understand that?"

Rain coming down a little harder. Said, "Reckon I got a right to know what I'm charged with."

He said, "Obstruction of justice, woman name of Dinkins picked up in Oklahoma confessed to killing a man in Cotterfield, got you deep implicated, boy. Time the grand jury's finished investigating good chance you'll be charged with accessory. Woman lives out on Mud creek says on the morning of August 28th she seen you drive off with the Dinkins woman, seen you back out there that night burying some dead dogs, be my guess that ain't all you buried." Didn't say nothing to that, wasn't nothing to say, he said, "Anything you want to get from the house?"

Done decided I didn't want no final farewells, said, "I reckon not."

He put the cuffs on me, led me over to the squad car, bout then's when I heard Henry calling my name. Looked down there, seen her and Harley standing at the side of the house, dim as ghosts in the falling rain.

Said to the sheriff, "It all right I say good-bye."

He give that a little thought, said, "All right, three minutes, we got you covered."

Went down there, hard to think just what to say, finally said, "Well, y'all look after yourselves." Didn't neither one of them say nothing, like me I reckon, didn't know what the hell to say. I said, "We got a good start on this farm, hard work, I know that, but anyways ain't nobody telling you what to do or when to do it. They's money in that account down town, nearly two thousand dollars left . . . ."

Harley said, "We'll look after Aunt Heather till you get out of the pen."

I said, "Well now, Harley, it ain't a absolute foregone certainty I'm going to be put in no pen." Knowed he meant well, said, "But I'm obliged to you all the same."

Stood a little longer, wasn't nothing else needed saying, I said, "Y'all hold her together, ain't nothing ever bad as it seems."

Started back up the rise, heard somebody running behind me, turned and seen Henry coming.

She got up there, stood a minute looking at me, said, "You was going off without saying nothing."

I said, "Well, I ain't much for goodbyes."

She looked out across the fields, rain running down her face, said, "How long will you be gone?"

I said, "I don't know. Know they can't pin no accessory charge on me, I never heard of nobody geting life for obstructing justice."

Still looking off at the fields, she said, "I'm going to miss you."

Ain't easy to say what you feel. Said, "Well, I ain't going to be gone forever."

She turned and looked at me, seen she wanted to say something but couldn't find words, then she come and put her arms around my neck and held tight. Wanted to hug her back but had them cuffs on, stood there feeling helpless, finally said, "Them men are waiting for me."

She let go, looked up at me, her lips pressed tight together, said, "I ain't going to cry."

I said, "Well, I thank you for that."

She turned and walked slow back down the rise, sheriff yelled, "All right, boy, let's go."

They put me in the car and drove away, got to the top of the rise I looked back, seen Harley and Henry blurred by rain standing at the corner of the house, still as stone, behind them dark skies and grey fields, jagged streaks of lighting above Butternut mountain. Looked more like a picture than something real.

Pordell

Went hard with me it come out at the trial I done time before, was a officer of the law myself when I liberated that daffy woman. They give me ten years, none of it suspended, guilty of conspiracy to obstruct a government operation. Been up here now seven months and some odd days, another year and one I take it to the Board.

Ain't exactly where I'd choose to be but better than last time. Captain Goddam's gone, ain't nobody yet declared open season on my scrawny ass. Things come my way, been here two weeks got assigned to the library, maybe the best work detail inside the walls, beats hell out of busting your balls working the pea patch. Gives me time to do some reading, write down what happened to me them few months I was out, maybe something to be learnt from that.

Nights is worst, laying there not able to sleep, listening to that poor lifer down the block playing them sorrowful tunes on his harp, counting footsteps when the guard makes his rounds. Times you get to nearly feeling sorry for yourself, which they ain't nothing worse than, knowing that ain't nothing but digging a hole to crawl into.

I reckon it's the farm that keeps me from the bane of self-pity, conjuring up scenes in my mind, that field growed up waist high in winter wheat, the pasture down along the creek green with sweet clover, them sheep grazing peaceful in the noonday sun.

Also thinking bout Harley and Henry, standing there in the rain the morning they carried me off. Long wearisome days we worked them fields, making something where they wasn't nothing before, times we sit on the back porch drinking beer and watching darkness come down. You're locked up, fighting stare fever, them's the things you think about. The gospel according to remembering the good times.

Another thing, you get to wondering sometimes if you was back in Cotterfield, had that woman in the car taking her to the county seat, would you do anything different. Truth is, I reckon I ain't learnt a hellova lot cause where I come out is I'd probably do the same thing I done last time. It's a fact I'm doing hard time but don't nothing trouble my sleep.

Henry writes pretty regular, handwriting so bad it sometimes takes me a while to decipher it, half the words mispelt, but day to day it's the one thing I look forward to. Last one she wrote said:

Dear Claude Dee,

   I hope you're doing all right. Me and Harley's fine.
He was on the roof of the backporch burning some
wasps nests and fell off on his head but he ain't hurt.
We sold twenty five bushel of turnips to the co-op in
town. We put them sheep in the lower pasture like
you said. We ain't bought a cow yet. Harley says cows
is dumb. We plowed under the wheat stubble and
planted soybeans. Mr. Ferguson come by ever day to
see we done it right. He says me and Harley is good
farmers. Sunday we went and got Aunt Heather like
always. I look forward to Sundays cause she comes
out. I got a calendar at the commissary so I can
mark off the days. In 407 days you'll be coming
home. That's all I think about.

                               Henry